HIDDEN FREEDOM

HIDDEN FREEDOM

CHARLES E. EADY

TRIPLE MEDIA

FLORIDA

Printed in the United States of America

Triple Media Publishing

Library of Congress Control Number 2018903081

ISBN 978-0-692-96193-3

Valerie Utton, editor

Alyssa Gamber-Ferrer, editor

Charles E. Eady, cover paintings

Available on amazon.com

Visit the website at deepersouth.org

TO MY FATHER, FAMILY

and SONS

Alex and Quinn

CONTENT

Introduction

It is a part of each of us——the desire to know something more about where we came from. We all have ancestors. We all came from the union of two people, and yet how many of us know their story?

The history our ancestors experienced was every bit as notable to them as our day-to-day life is for us.

What follows is the story about a tri-racial settlement in South Carolina, where African Americans, Native Americans and Whites lived together in Berkeley County. It appears the Africans journeyed to the new world in the bottom of Spanish ships; they revolted against their oppressors to gain their freedom in 1526. It was the first slave revolt on American soil.

Much of our "popular" history focuses on the journey and struggles of African Americans. Because of that, there are few historical accounts of Africans and Native American

Indians whose lives during that time entwined. These groups in the South were given names such as Brass Ankles, Red Bones, Lumbee, and Turks.

Most of us are aware of the freedom Native American Indians had, however, few of us know that according to federal census documents from 1790 to 1860. *There were more free blacks living in the South than the North. Furthermore, there were nearly twice as many owning properties in the South than the North. Source: Ira Berlin, Slaves Without Masters.*

By 1860, nearly 10,000 free blacks and mulattoes lived in South Carolina and about 500,000 in America.

There were many laws written about the rights free blacks should—or shouldn't—have that varied from state to state. Private citizens often wrote their legislators to petition for laws that would address issues and concerns about the "balance" they wished to see maintained in their community regarding free blacks.

The documents throughout this book provides reasons to question history that has been presented as facts. American history presents itself on its own terms about free blacks. They owned land, wrote wills, went to court and were counted on the census. They were entitled to—and had—rights before slavery ended.

This is a fictional story based on a collection of true documents, by these documents, the book, "Hidden Freedom," reveals an unknown south.

About the Author

Charles Eady a graduate of Claflin University, is an artist and educator whose search for information about his family's history started in 2008 after watching a PBS series hosted by Henry Louis Gates. Through the program, Charles learned that many historical documents were accessible and was immediately inspired to look deeper into his own family history. Before too long, he started uncovering documents that exposed both facts and details about the South that were unlike the history lessons he'd been taught in school.

When he realized that authors, historians, and universities had already researched the Eady surname because of its African and Indian connections. He expanded his research to learn more about the time periods during which his ancestors had lived, hoping to learn more about their lives—and perhaps even uncover more of their written history.

"The research was to provide my father with information about our family, until I saw a 1790 census listing "other free" families living in the South with our surname. I never knew free blacks lived in the South and didn't think they would have been counted on the censuses. Being a teacher, I knew I was seeing rear history that was not included in school textbooks. It made me want to learn more."

One of the more interesting documents Charles found early on was his surname on a transcribed copy of the first census of St. Johns Parish, Berkeley County, South Carolina, that had a column titled, "All other free persons." It was an inspiring find, but it left him a bit skeptical, and he became captivated with finding more supporting documentation between his surname and "All other free persons." In his role as an educator, he also came across a textbook, which stated that all blacks who lived in the South were slaves; because of his research, he knew this statement was false. That too fueled him to look deeper.

"I wanted to tell their stories about the South. From then on, when I saw a land grant, or a person listed as head of household I didn't assume it was a white person, nor did I assume their racial attitudes towards each other, I relied on records, documents and credible sources. Then I began to put a conversation together as it may have sounded."

Two more of Charles's more inspiring finds were: tax returns of free blacks who were required to pay a two-dollar capitation tax due to a law passed in 1792 and seeing a map from 1895 showing a town named Eadytown. Perhaps the most startling find over the years was the fact that there were free blacks who owned slaves for economical gain. Yet, as Carter G. Woodson presented in his book, it was often a matter of purchasing their family members out of slavery.

Charles's research continued for nine years. During that time, he used his formal skills as an artist to create a collection of paintings based on an artistic integration of the documents he'd found. His goal was to exhibit the paintings and share the truths he was uncovering.

After several successful exhibits, people began to share how inspired they'd been to research their own family histories. Many suggested he write a book to reach a larger audience.

Charles also gave presentations about his research, and at the end of one of his presentations, a genealogist in attendance asked him, "What are you going to do with all this information?"

It was a good question and coupled with the responses he'd gotten from his exhibits, Charles acknowledged that a book would be a good way to share what he'd learned about these long-hidden documents about the South.

This book reveals a broader view of the South and integrates facts with insights and interpretations about what it might have been like to be both free and black in the early days of South Carolina.

Acknowledgments

Thanks to God on all accounts. My two awesome sons for feedback. Alex my youngest who coped with a decade of me writing on this project and helping with formatting issues.

I was fortunate to have Valarie Utton as the lead editor.

It was first written as a screen play for a movie, an idea introduced by Steven Haynes and typed into a screen play by Kimberly Hamilton.

Scott Mitchell of the Silver River Museum for my first presentation on the topic. Lee Swartz, the branch manager of Belleview's main library arranged a presentation. The Webber Museum at Central Florida College who displayed my first exhibit with the controversial paintings. Jacksonville, FL main library for extending an exhibit.

Claflin University in Orangeburg, SC held an exhibit titled, HIDDEN FREEDOM at the Authur Rose Museum, curated by Xan Jennings. Adonnica Toler and Lydia Stewart displayed several paintings at the Ritz Museum, in Jacksonville, FL as a part of their, "Through our Eyes", exhibit, and Peter Schreyer for an invitation to show at the Creald'e School of Arts in Orlando, Fl.

Forest Hazel a historian at NC Chapel Hill University for his in-depth study of Native Americans, including the

Eady surname which was the foundation of my early research. The many librarians who helped find related books. The Main Library in Columbia, SC for sending, SC Indians, Indian traders, and other ethnic connections, beginning in 1670, by Theresa M. Hicks to Ocala, FL.

Katrina Vitcus a teacher at Dunnelon High School for helping with formatting. Teachers at Sunrise Elementary, Karen Blinkhorn, Kelly Asquith and Angela Jewell who encouraged me to write this book. Marion Oaks Middle School, Sylvia Culbreath. Belleview High School, Beth Inman, Debbie Callahan and Lt. McCormick. Jacquelyn Fields who read an early version of the manual script. Sonya Williams for helping with editing.

Julie Bateman a graduate of Belleview HS was the first to type it as a book. David Reedy another graduate of Belleview HS, read it as a screenplay and made valuable suggestions. Kylah Gardner and Rebecca Bernier helped with editing. Emily Bennett, Makala Moody, Christina Messer, Sierra Watkins student readers who gave suggestions. Sofia Ingersoll, Myles Monroe, Anthony Raymond, Au'je Middleton, Kristen Lee, Maria Rodriquez, Britney Terrell and Jamie, students who helped with ideas and interest. Also, to the many students who would ask, "How's the book going?

1895 Eadytown map. Source: Rand McNally.

Eadytown, a post-village of Berkeley county, SC. Population about 75.

Source: Lippincott Gazetteer of the World.

Chapter 1

Hostile Waters

Spanish ships sail towards a coast of land to one day be known as Carolina. The sails surrender to the wind as raging waters clash against the hulls of the ships. A steady flow of blue-grey waves ripple along the shore.

A man wearing rugged Spanish apparel, is jumping up and down at the front of the ship because of what he sees.

Lucas Vasquez de Allyon, the captain, stands on the forward deck of the tallest ship with his eyes looking to the horizon. He is about 50 years old and spiritedly short. He impatiently holds out his hand to wait for his telescope. Once he feels the thrust of it hitting his hand, he swiftly lifts it to his jumpy right eye, closing the other to get a clear view.

He stands as still as the ships mast as he surveys the coast, his beard is deep black and dabbled with gray, perfectly groomed and the only part of him moving in the breeze. He sees a shoreline of tawny brown sand giving way to a magnificent landscape piercing the lens of his telescope. A small smile curls one corner of his mouth, he has sailed distant waters in search of this shore.

Below the deck of the middle ship are shackled Bantu slaves eating their rationed breakfast. The Bantu slaves can hear the shouts above and realize they must be approaching land; they see the early morning sunlight peeking through the open door leading up and out of the hold.

Standing on the deck of the ship the crew stares with awe at a shore covered with palmetto trees. Many are sailors who haven't seen land or their families for over a year. The others are settlers, men and women who have come to a new land for a better life. As well as a Catholic priest, who came to dedicate the land to Spain.

Tristan, the first mate is running across the deck yelling as loud as he can. "We are approaching land! Oy…OY…. Ready the anchors!"

As the ships draw closer to shore, unrelenting heat takes hold of the day, a countless number of gnats parade through the air. The humidity turns every movement into an effort and the captain wipes his brow but regards the conditions as nothing more than a small nuisance. His mind is on the gratitude and recognition he will receive from King Charles.

Captain Lucas Vasquez de Allyon motions to Tristan who yells out commands for the crew to hoist the anchors off the deck and into the water.

Tristan shouts again and the crew goes quiet as the captain steps up to the highest point on the deck and declares, "Gentlemen! Over the Beast of the Sea, we have traveled to reach this land to claim it for our King!"

The crew cheers and several of them move to the longboats to take their captain to the smallest ship.

When he is aboard, he commands them to raise the anchors and sail the small ship into the mouth of the river. The tide joins them, and the river smoothly pushes the ship further up the wide river channel.

The birds in the trees take to the air, their loud songs are a protest to the intrusion, wild boars retreat from the shore like wildebeest being chased by hungry lions.

The captain picks his mark and shouts, "We will cast our anchors here and set our feet upon this new land." When the captain feet are firm, and his crew joins his side he declares, "In the name of King Charles, in the year *1526* this settlement will be called San Miguel de Gualdape." He then orders a flag in the ground and a cannon to be fired.

As another longboat approach the shore, Tristan jumps up and runs to the Captain, he points to something in the near distance. A wild boar, dead, an arrow shaft pointing out of it. "We have company Captain."

"Company with a good aim," the captain replied. A crewmember from the longboat extends his trembling hand and shouts, "Captain! Look!"

Both the Captain and Tristan look in the direction he is pointing. "The land is revealing more of its wild inhabitants," the captain remarks as the Catawba Indians make their way towards them.

They are moving swiftly some on horseback and some on foot. As they get closer the black circles around their left eyes became noticeable, they were painted during their battle ceremony. The captain knew this because his brother Gordillo told him of this custom. By the triumphant looks on their faces, they had won their battle.

The Indian leader raises his hand and make a tight fist, pulling his warriors to a complete stop a small distant away from the captain and his crew. The mighty force of Catawba Indians are directly in front of Allyon and his crew.

A deep silence stretches between the Spaniards and the Indians. The birds are quiet, and the land is silent except for the sounds of a few impatient horses.

The fierce copper-toned and muscular Indian leader broke the stillness of the moment, speaking in his native language. "Ships like yours have been to our land before. They took those who were without weapons while our warriors were away. Tell me, why you have returned to our land. Do you think you will once again leave with our people?"

The captain is reluctant to say a word. He doesn't speak this language; his mind is assessing all options. The Indians are too close, and his crewmember's guns are too far away.

The captain turned to Tristan. "Have them bring Chiaro at once," he says.

Tristan turns around and heads back to the ship, anchored just off the shore. He shouts to crewmembers on deck to bring Chiaro to shore.

Chiaro is below deck, where he has been for a long time. He can hear noises, but not well enough to know what's going on. As footsteps near, he gets nervous. Then, one of the crewmembers stood in front of him.

"Get up. The Captain is calling for you!"

Chiaro stands up calmly. He is grabbed by the arm and hurried up the stairs into a small boat that quickly rows to shore. Tristan takes him to stand by the captain. Chiaro remains calm, now he understands. The captain has called him to be his interpreter.

He immediately recognizes his brother the Indian leader, of the Catawba Nation, that stretches across the Carolina low country. Etiwan immediately recognizes Chiaro, neither of them says anything to let anyone know.

Lucas Vasquez de Allyon had told Gordillo to develop a good relationship with the inhabitants of the land. Instead, Captain Gordillo conspired with a slave hunter and enslaved many Indians in the encounter Etiwan spoke of to the captain.

Captain Gordillo returned to Hispaniola with the slaves. When they arrived, Lucas Vasquez de Allyon demanded they be set free. He was impressed with how well Chiaro spoke the English language he'd learned from English fur trappers who'd made frequent trips to the Carolinas, so he'd kept him as an interpreter.

Later, he took Chiaro to meet the Queen of Spain. She was also impressed with Chiaro's fluency with the English language. Now, Chiaro was once again on Indian soil, face-to-face with his native people.

The captain instructs Chiaro to tell the Indian leader, "We only want to stay for a few days to build peaceful relations so that we may learn from their culture," and, "It would benefit both our people with trades," and, "We come in peace."

"Hmm," mused Etiwan. "Would that be a piece of our land, or all of it?"

Chiaro began to speak to Etiwan in their native language. "It is good to see you Brother, it has been so many years. I do not know their intentions."

"How have you been treated?" Etiwan asked.

"I have been treated well because of my knowledge of their language."

Etiwan, the Indian leader, looks directly at the captain. "We have not seen any friendliness from your ships or your people. Years ago, your people took many of our sisters and brothers on your ship. They never returned to their homeland. Do you have any knowing of this, Captain?"

Chiaro interprets Etiwan's words, and the captain tries to put the Indian leader at ease, choosing his words cautiously. "I ensure you they were set free; my brother led the expedition, and he did not follow my command to establish a friendly relationship with your people. At my command, all who were enslaved became free citizens of Hispaniola."

Etiwan says, "I know in fact you do not speak the truth. My brother is your interpreter, enslaved on that ship years ago. Release him, or you will have an unkind fate. My people number in the thousands and we are a mighty nation."

The captain shrugged. "He is a free man. If he wants to return to his people, he can."

Tristan immediately let Chiaro go to stand with his native people. A horse of strong stature is lead to him, and he effortlessly jumps onto the bare back.

"We offer you our fattest pigs in return for a short stay," said the captain.

Chiaro spoke to Etiwan while staring at the captain. "They have many slaves in the lower decks, as well as horses."

Etiwan lifts his hands and starts to speak, while Chiaro translates his words. "In exchange for the horses you have aboard, I will let you stay upon our land for a while. I warn you though, the unsheltered conditions will siege upon you before the approaching winter. You will come to know if your blood is able to battle against the sickness of the mosquitoes."

When Chiaro finishes, Etiwan turns to him and said, "The slaves must gain their own freedom."

Chiaro was silent, he understood.

As the Carolina sky gave way to the deepening of dusk, the Catawba nation ride off in a display of absolute power. The Indians ride their new Spanish horses, making battle sounds. The horses' hooves thud the ground, the horses thrill to be on land.

The next morning, the first European colony on American soil begin, San Miguel de Gualdape. The

Bantu slaves wear loose fitting Spanish clothes. They carry the lumber, tools, and supplies from the ships to the nearby site, and build according to the skills they learned from their elders, their African influences apparent in details such as dovetail connections. Since the Spanish crewmembers have no knowledge of the Bantu language and are content with the fact that they aren't required to take on the labor, they let the slaves continue according to their own craftsmanship.

The settlers help with the building. A few ventures out on their own up the Pee Dee River and deeper into Indian Territory and were never seen again.

Three months later, as Etiwan had foretold, the captain and many of his crew, along with the settlers become gravely ill, even more have died. Early one morning, the remaining healthy crewmembers gather around the captain. They are wondering why they have been summoned.

"When we began building this settlement three month ago, I was in perfect health," the captain said speaking his words barely above a sickly whisper. "Now I am deeply ill, and do not know if it was a good decision to have stayed to build this settlement. My brother unsuccessfully surveyed the land, his concern had been finding slaves. Now, many of the crewmen and settlers are perishing."

"At night, I can hear many of you fighting about who will become captain. I have decided Tristan will be your captain, as well as the leader of this new colony if I do not recover. He has been trustworthy and loyal since our departure and has not fallen into contests aimed at my position."

Tristan watches as his captain quickly tires, his eyes sliding shut, and turns to the men gathered around. "You've heard what the captain had to say, now it's time you got back to your positions."

At noon, Etiwan and Chiaro ride into the settlement. They vault from their horses and stand before Tristan. "We have word that your captain is ill with the fever," Chiaro said. "Where is he?"

They walk into a makeshift tent where the captain is resting, many sheets cover his stricken body. He has noticeably lost weight and has a look of despair at never seeing the settlement he'd started completed.

Tristan speaks quietly to Chiaro and Etiwan, "This settlement could build a good relationship between your people and my people. If this colony continues, other Spaniards will come and bring good trade to your land."

"What you say sounds good for my people; however, it would not be probable because of our different beliefs about human equality," Chiaro says, knowing that the words Etiwan had spoken on that first day, the words that had given the captain protection from other Indians while he built his colony, would end if the captain dies.

Chiaro turns away and slowly walks through the settlement towards the outer edge where the Bantu slaves stay. There he saw Balipho, the leader of the Bantu slaves. The two men regard each other; they both know the meaning of being a slave.

Chiaro isn't skill with the Bantu language, he stops walking and speaks to Balipho in subtle gestures. "Your people and my people share similar beliefs in our cultures. When you and your people decide you are ready to strike against your oppressors," Chiaro says, shifting just his eyes in the direction of the woods, "you will find many hatchets at the edge of the wood. When you are free, you can find shelter among my people."

A few days later, soon after the night had claimed the day, a few Bantu slaves sat in a small circle. Balipho stood in the middle of the human circle, a small fire burns next to him, every Bantu eye focuses on him.

Two Spanish crewmembers stand in the distance watching the circle of slaves from the shadows of the newly constructed building as their guns rest against the wall.

"Mosquito bites make the Spaniards burn with fever," Balipho says in a courageous but quiet voice as he slaps a mosquito on his arm. "We must have medicine in our veins."

"Are the Spaniards sick enough for us to escape?" one of the slaves asks.

"Our Indian friends have left weapons at the edge of the woods. Inaha, you and Dongola will find and gather them." Balipho stops. He doesn't look towards the Spanish crewmembers; he knows they are watching. "The Spaniards do not consider us capable of planning a victorious attack. Those that have survived the fever are the strongest, but we will be triumphant. Who among us can move swiftly to gather their guns without awakening them?"

Several slaves make small but noticeable motions. Balipho signals his approval. Each of them were fierce hunters in their African homeland.

"At dawn of the new day, we will attack. We will show them our skills and courage to defeat them. We will be as brave as lions protecting their pride," Balipho declares battle.

As the slaves walk away, Balipho sit, planning for the next morning. They had gathered the guns, and all were asleep now, except for him. He thought of his family in Africa, knowing that he would never see them again. He felt comfort in knowing they would live together in the unity of freedom. He watches for the horizon to show the first pale signs of morning and began to awaken the Bantu slaves.

The same two crewmembers who'd been on watch the night before had fallen asleep, one of them woke by the repeated bites of mosquitoes. Seeing the Bantu slaves gathering themselves together, some with hatchets, some with guns, in their hand, he stands and yell to the men while looking around for his gun. "Get back to your quarters!"

Balipho, with his mighty voice no longer restrained, violently screams, "ATTACK!"

The Bantu slaves use their weapons to battle the Spaniards in remembrance of freedom. They fight for freedom on this new land, rising against their oppressors, determined to regain their independence.

"To arms men!" Tristan yells as he exits his tent and takes in what's happening. The guards and crewmembers reach for their missing guns. Panic spreads like fire on dry wood while the Bantu slaves charge forward.

Tristan runs towards the ship to alert the crewmembers. Balipho sees where he's running and understands what he's going to do, he deftly maneuvers himself through the battle to follow him. When Tristan reaches the shore, he looks for the guard who should be standing at the bow of the ship but doesn't see him. "Ahoy!" Tristan screams.

Balipho reaches the shore. Tristan senses danger and swings around. They stand, too far apart to reach each other, but close enough to know what the other has in mind.

Tristan can hear noises coming from the ship and is relieved to know that the guard must have raised the alarm. There were still guns on the boat. All he needs is a little time.

Balipho raises his hatchet and takes a step forward determined that Tristan would not shout again.

Tristan realizes he doesn't stand a chance and motions for Balipho to put his weapon down so they can fight man-to-man. Balipho shakes his head no. He knows there are men with guns on the ships.

Tristan catches sight of a sailor with a gun standing behind Balipho. Once again, Tristan feels a wink of relief as the man raises the gun to take aim.

Then he sees a Bantu slave aiming at the sailor. The slave pulls the trigger first, hitting the sailor on the left side of his chest, but he still manages to pull the trigger before falling to the ground.

The shot shrills between the two men. It was never Balipho's plan for his people to do anything other than to escape. They had accomplished their goal of letting the Spaniards know they were no longer slaves. Balipho shouts to his people, "Escape to the woods!"

Tristan dashes around Balipho, and make a run for the fallen sailors' gun, by the time he had it, Balipho was out of sight. As he looks around at the chaos in camp, he can see the Bantu slaves starting to take refuge into the woods.

Scouts race back to the Catawba Indians to report what is happening. They gather a force of men, and hurry to the settlement, hearing shots as they are approaching. From a distance, Chiaco can see the slaves retreating into the woods he stops and doesn't approach. "Once there were many more Spaniards than Bantus. Now the Bantus aren't as outnumbered," he says as he starts to motion his warriors forward.

However, Etiwan stops him. "No Brother. This is their battle."

Tristan stares at the settlement. Men lay everywhere—some wounded and moaning, some clearly dead. Even if he had the forces to chase the slaves into the woods, he didn't know who might be waiting for them. He could see, Etiwan and Chiaro watching from a distance, with their warriors.

By the time it was fully daylight, Tristan could fully see the devastation. There had been 600 crewmembers on the banks of the Pee Dee River. The fever epidemic decreased their ranks down to a mere 200. Moreover, he'd lost over 100 men in the Bantu revolt.

Captain Tristan returned with his remaining crew to Hispaniola, with only memories of the short-lived colony near the mouth of the Pee Dee River.

William Katz coined the term Black Indians in his book, Black Indians a Hidden Heritage, 1986.

The Black Indians of the Pee Dee River became the first colony on this continent to practice the belief that all people-newcomer and native are created equal and are entitles to life, liberty, and the pursuit of happiness.

Chapter 2

Brass Ankle Families

After the Catawba Indians welcome the once Bantu slaves, they become a mixed-race along the banks of the Pee Dee River. The two races find they share a mutual respect of the land and have similar customs and ways of singing and dancing. The Catawba soon realize there is something within the blood of the Bantu's that protect them from malaria. The Catawba women begin to choose Bantu men to prevent their offspring's from getting the disease. These unions result in this settlement becoming predominately-Negro blood.

William Pocher gives an account of his travels in Transactions of the Huguenot Society of South Carolina, Issues 10-14.

Traveling through a dense forest with occasional glimpses of the reservoirs of the Santee Canal we come to Eady Town, once the seat of a village of half breeds...

Daniel once lived on this settlement, he rides with caution through the morning fog until he reaches the courthouse. Once inside he walks down a long hallway seeking the office that issues land grants. A sign hangs above a closed door. He enters the small room and sees a woman wearing a white dress and horn-rimmed glasses standing behind a long table.

In Colonial South Carolina, land was granted under various laws and statutes as decreed by the king of England and/or the Lords Proprietors. Any free person could appear before the Council and petition for a survey to be granted land.... After the petition for a survey was submitted, the person appeared before the Council and petitioned for a grant to pass which authorized the surveyor to measure out the land.

It is believed that property was awarded by land grants to persons who were either all or part Native American who acquired land in this manner. Such a man was Daniel Eddy who was known to be a Revolutionary War soldier and cobbler....

Source: Dr. Vanik Eaddy genealogy study.

"How do Ma'am," said Daniel.

"Good day," she says with a British accent."

Daniel takes off the brown hat he only wears to conduct business, or go to church, and hangs it on a hook behind the door. He is holding a folded paper—a decree made by King George that allows him to petition for land. "There is a plat of land in St. Johns Parish I'd like to petition for, to work and harvest with my family."

The clerk takes the offered paper. "You'll have to go through the regular statutes of decree. Meanwhile, I'll take down your information and make a warrant for the land. What is your first and last name?"

"Daniel Eady."

"A thoughtful look arrives on her face. "Your name seems familiar. Are you part Indian?"

"I hear that whenever I come to town. Most of my family live near the Pee Dee River. I moved to St. Johns Parish several years ago."

The clerk is interested because she's heard stories about Africans living among Indians, who were given derogatory names like brass ankles.

She continues to take down Daniel information, and then reads it back to him. "This is a petition to ask his Excellency, King George, to send surveyors to mark, and set forth a land grant for 100 acres to be worked by me, my wife, my children, and two slaves."

The clerk reads to Daniel the papers that will be filed, she lowers her head and looks at him over the rim of her glasses. *"The petitioner appeared and was sworn to the truth of his said family, on this 21*[st] *day of January in the year of our Lord 1773.*

Do you agree?" "Yes Ma'am."

She shakes her head in approval. "This prayer will be granted, and the deputy surveyor will prepare a warrant to pursuant, to run out the 100 acres mentioned." Then you will return here in two months to appear before the council for a final decision."

"I'll make sure I'm here. Have a good day Ma'am," he says as he retrieves his hat.

Daniel Eddy petitioned for a plot of land in 1773 to Great Britain. Source: South Carolina Department of Archives and History. A copy of the original petition is on the following page.

572

SOUTH-CAROLINA.

GEORGE the *Third* by the Grace of God, of GREAT-BRITAIN, FRANCE and IRELAND, KING, Defender of the Faith, and so forth, To ALL to whom THESE PRE-SENTS SHALL come GREETING: KNOW YE, THAT WE of our special Grace, certain Knowledge and mere Motion, have given and granted, and by these Presents, for us our heirs and successours, DO GIVE AND GRANT unto *Daniel Eddy his* heirs and assigns, a plantation or tract of land containing *One hundred acres in St. John's Parish Berkley County bounding South West on Henry Winningham, North West on Samuel Richbourg North East on Peter Brelier South East on vacant lands. &c.*

And hath such shape, form and marks, as appear by a plat thereof, hereunto annexed: Together with all woods, under-woods, timber and timber-trees, lakes, ponds, fishings, waters, water-courses, profits, commodities, appurtenances and hereditaments whatsoever, thereunto belonging or in anywise appertaining: Together with privilege of hunting, hawking and fowling in and upon the same, and all mines and minerals whatsoever; saving and reserving, nevertheless, to us, our heirs and successours, all white pine-trees, if any there should be found growing thereon; and also saving and reserving, nevertheless, to us, our heirs and successours, one tenth-part of mines of gold and silver only: TO HAVE AND TO HOLD, the said tract of *One hundred* acres of land and all and singular other the premises hereby granted unto the said *Daniel Eddy his* heirs and assigns for ever, in free and common socage, the said *Daniel Eddy his* heirs and assigns yielding and paying therefor unto us, our heirs and successours, or to our Receiver-General for the time being, or to his Deputy or Deputies for the time being, yearly, that is to say, on *the* twenty-fifth day of March, in every year at the rate of three shillings sterling, or four shillings proclamation money, for every hundred acres, and so in proportion, according to the *number* of acres, contained herein; the same to commence at the expiration of *two* years from the date hereof. Provided always, and this present Grant is upon condition, nevertheless, that the said *Daniel Eddy his* heirs or assigns, shall and do, yearly, and every year, on and after the date of these presents, clear and cultivate at the rate of *three* acres for every hundred acres of land, and such proportion according to the number of acres herein contained; AND ALSO shall and do enter a minute or docket of these our letters patent in the office of our Auditor-General for the time being, in our said Province, within *ten* months from the date hereof; AND upon condition, that if the said rent, hereby reserved, shall happen to be in arrear and unpaid for the space of *three* years from the time it shall become due, and no distress can be found on the said lands, tenements and hereditaments hereby granted; or if the said *Daniel Eddy his* heirs or assigns shall neglect to clear and cultivate yearly and every year, at the rate of *three* acres for every hundred acres of land, and so in proportion, according the number of acres herein contained, or if a minute or docket of these our letters patent, shall not be entered in the office of our Auditor-General for the time being, in our said Province, within *eight* months from the date hereof, that then and in any of these cases, this present Grant shall cease, and determine and be utterly void; and the said lands, tenements and hereditaments hereby granted, and every part and parcel thereof, shall revert to us, our heirs and successours, as fully and absolutely, as if the same had never been granted.

Given under the Great Seal of our said Province.

WITNESS *the Hon.ble William Bull Esq. L.t* Governor and Commander in chief in and over our said Province of South-Carolina, this *Thirty-first* Day of *August* Anno Dom. 17*75* in the *fourteenth* Year of our Reign.

William (L. M. S.) *Bull*

Signed by the *Governor the Lieut.*

Governor in Council

Tho. Winstanley p. Co.

And hath thereunto a plat there of annexed, representing the same, certified by

John Bremar D.y Surveyor-General.
March 15.th 1773.

SOUTH CAROLINA

GEORGE the third by the Grace of God, of Great- Britain, France and Ireland, King, Defender of the Faith, and forth, To ALL TO WHOM THESE PRESENTS SHALL COME GREETING: know ye that we of our special grace, certain Knowledge and were Motion, have given and granted, and by these presents, for us our heirs and seccessers, DO GIVE AND GRANT UNTO

Daniel Eddy his heirs and assigns, a plantation or trace of land containing *one hundred acres in the St. Johns Parish Berkeley County bounding in South Carolina west on Henry Winningham north west on Samuel Richosing north east on Peter Coutrier and south east on vacant land.*

March 15, 1773

Transcribed from the land grant of Daniel Eddy.

Daniel prepares the soil for planting; he has been growing crops in St. Johns Parish for seventeen years. Daniel is a tall man with a commanding presence, he plows the land with the help of his 12-year-old nephew Bristow.

Bristow is thin and long limbed. He likes to visit his uncle, because he likes working hard and listening to his uncle stories. Even at this early age, he focuses on the task, his mind is set with resolve as his calloused hands move with usefulness.

They till the field urging on a sluggish ox under the toiling heat, preparing the soil to plant cottonseeds. The intensity of the afternoon heat eases as the day fades, draining their energy along the way.

Daniel takes off his work hat and wipes the sweat from his face with a rag that he pulls out of his back pocket, it grips his coarse skin.

Then Bristow reaches to pull a rag from his pocket. To get it, he carefully shifts the hatchet that's hanging from a loop. He'd been waiting on this hatchet since he was eight years old after learning what it stood for. It was a hatchet from the Pee Dee River revolt passed down to him when he turned twelve. He'd finally gotten it three days earlier at a family gathering, and he'd been wearing it with pride ever since.

"Uncle Daniel," he asks with youthful eagerness, "how did we get all this land?"

"Well, since we're done working, and you are getting older, this might be a good time to tell you how this land became a part of our family. This is the story of your Uncle John who was in the Revolutionary War. You've heard about the war with the British and about what they wanted."

Bristow nods.

"Well, one night some Indians sat in a teepee as darkness began to settle. A fire was burning in their midst. "We all know what the Red Coats want," your Uncle John said. "They want our land."

"A few days later, a Lieutenant named Francis Marion arrived in the area, some people knew him as "The Swamp Fox." They called him that because he fought his battles using successful, but uncommon strategies. He'd gone there looking for volunteers to join the fight against the British."

"The weather was rough." A sodden rain had been falling mostly all day, farmers, soaked to the skin, showed up to do their part. The Lieutenant sat under a tent with a few soldiers, while newly enlisted soldiers practiced battle maneuvers in the rain and the mud.

"When your Uncle John joined the line, he knew he was standing with good men. He could tell most of them were farmers, because they came dressed in their farming clothes wanting to fight, they're worrying about their families they're leaving behind which stopped some from joining."

"When your uncle reached the front of the line, a soldier in uniform asked him, "Do you understand this battle could last for years?"

"I will fight for this land until the war ends," your Uncle John said.

"The soldier looked at him hard. "How will you provide for your family while you're gone?"

"My son is twelve. He can fire a musket and has a good aim for squirrels and my wife is good at keeping things going."

The Lieutenant liked that he is concerned about his family and seemed like a man of good character. "Good. He can shoot squirrels and you will be home for dinner. You see, this unit will fight as soldiers during the day, and return home as farmers in the evening."

"As your uncle turned and walked away, Lt. Marion—who grew up in the same area as your uncle—got up and followed him.

"John," he called, "I haven't seen you since we built the Bogey Creek Bridge."

"This is a good strategy you have… to use farmers who know the area to fight against the Red Coats," your uncle said.

"My method is simple. It's the same method as building a bridge—use good materials. He looks at John earnestly. "You know there is very little pay."

"My ancestors have lived on this land for many generations. The pay is to preserve our land and our ways."

Weeks later, Lt. Marion walked into the center of a cleared-out area and stepped onto the stump of a sawed-down oak tree. His uniform was marred with the signs of battle, but a look of determination quickly drew his soldiers around him. "I know these woods like a saddle knows a horse. We may be outnumbered, but I assure you that we will defeat the Red Coats. We will strike them before they know we are coming."

"There were a few times when your uncle was able to come home, but not many. Like it was for so many of the men who had enlisted, home was miles away, so they stayed at the camp and trained and prepared for the battle they knew were coming. That night, after Lt. Marion had spoken, your uncle stayed and did what all the other men did—ate supper, talked about strategy and victory, cleaned his rifle, checked his ammunition, and slept under the shelter of the thick canopy of the tall oak.

"The next morning, the heat began with the sun. Uncle John said it was so hot that even the flapjacks were sweating. When he was finished eating, a soldier came up to him and told him that Lt. Marion wanted to see him.

"John," Lt. Marion started, "I want you to take four men with you and find out where the British soldiers are, and then get back here as quickly as you can. If you're caught, the men will tell them you're a runaway slave being returned."

"Your uncle left with the other four soldiers and didn't return for a few days. Finally, the five tired men slowly walked across the field. As they approached, the soldiers saw your uncle carrying rabbits, two in each hand. He handed them off, then was immediately taken to see Lt. Marion.

"The British are marching towards Eutaw Springs," he said.

"Soon thereafter, what every soldier had been waiting for had arrived. It was the morning of their attack; the fog was heavy, and the Swamp Fox was pleased as he led his army through the swamp towards the back of the British camp. He knew the swamp like a saddle knows a horse, he was glad for the fog and how well it would hide their approach and they'd be able to get closer without being spotted."

"He also knew the British wouldn't expect an attack to come from the swamp. He could tell by the smells blowing in their direction that the British were having breakfast. They'd be on the lookout for an attack alright, from the opposite direction."

"It was still very early in the morning and the closer they got to the camp, the lighter the fog got. A British lookout balanced between branches of a tall tree spotted the men coming through the swamp. The lookout focused his eyes on Lt. Marion. "The Swamp Fox is in the swamp!" he yelled.

"Lt. Marion heard the lookout and as soon as he caught sight of him in the tree, he shot at him. Of course, the rest of the British soldiers heard the shot. They dropped their breakfast, grabbed their rifles, and ran to form battle lines in front of a field of thick pine trees at the edge of the swamp.

"Lt. Marion shouted to his men, "Stay near the trees! Move up and keep firing!" His men continued to advance; now they were being shot at. Soon enough, the gunshots slowed down. British soldiers were shot while they were reloading. Others were shot because their rifles were jammed. They kept hold of their rifles because they had bayonets on the ends. As Marion's men got closer, they started fighting man-to-man."

"Some of our men were shot. One of the scouts your uncle went scouting with was one of them. As he fell to the ground, Lt. Marion shot the British soldier responsible and shouted to his men. "We are the last force of opposition to the British! Let us make this a victorious battle!"

"A British soldier aimed for Lt. Marion. He had a clear shot, but one of the Lieutenant's men who'd been shot still had his rifle and shot at the British soldier. He missed, but his shot alerted Lt. Marion who turned and shot the British soldier himself.

"The battle lasted until nightfall, and many men died, it was the British soldiers who were defeated in this battle. Your Uncle John continued to be a part of the fight against the British. When the war ended in 1787, the colonies claimed their independence as a new nation, your Uncle was honored for his services and was awarded a plot of land. He worked hard, to grow corn and cabbage for his first-year harvest."

"I petitioned Great Britain for land before the war. As you know, it's a lot of land, and a lot of work. I know this is hard work, but it will give you a notion to work hard for what you want. Remember, it's family who live on this land, and this land is a part of you. And by all means, you are to fight for your land!" Daniel said looking towards the darkened horizon. "Let's get back to the house. It's time for dinner."

Negroes fought with Allen's Green Mountain Boys and were members of the guerrilla fighters led in South Carolina by Francis Marion.

...At least one South Carolina Negro, John Eady, also distinquished himself in the Revolutionary Army and was rewarded with land and freedom.

Source: Herbert Aptheker, the author of, The American Revolution 1763-1783.

"Forgotten Patriots: African American and American Indian Patriots in the Revolutionary War," by Eric Grundset. List John Eady as an African American hero in South Carolina during the Revolutionary War.

Around noon the next day, Daniel and Bristow are once again working in the field. Their dogs down by the house begin to bark and the two of them stop working. Bristow points at two men slowly riding horses approaching the settlement. "Who are those men?"

Daniel looks towards the trail and studies the men. He doesn't know them, and it's the first time unknown white people have ever been on his property. Daniel is calm, but takes the approach of the men with caution, and walks down to the house.

He stands in front of his house with his hands cross on top of a pitchfork plunge into the ground. He waits as the men walk their horses up the long dirt trail to the house. As they get closer, a small dog starts runs towards them.

"Get back here Ribsy!" Daniel commands. Ribsy runs back and settles at Daniels side. "Well now, I have never seen y'all in these parts before, we don't get unexpected visitors around here. So, what brings you to the lowlands? Are you collecting taxes, or looking for runaways?" Daniel asks.

Bristow walks up and stands behind his uncle so he can hear what's being said.

"No Sir," the oldest man says while pulling a bulky leather-bound journal out of his saddlebag. "We're here conducting the very first census in America. My name is Colburn. This is Johnson, and it's our first time in these parts. Our job is to go down every crook and cranny and count every person we find. We saw this trail leading into the woods, so we followed it and ended up here."

Colburn pushes back the straw hat that he's wearing so his face isn't hidden. "The work is tiring, and I'm sure we'll miss plenty of people who live in these hard to get to places, figuring out how many people live in South Carolina is important work. Sometimes it's a little dangerous. Some of our marshals have been warned to stay away or get shot."

Daniel is a little wary about the strangers and surveys them closely. Colburn looks to be about 45 years old and has a dark scrubby mustache. Both men's clothes are dusty. Johnson's eyes are nervously flickering around the property, which is an untrustworthy way to be handling himself in Daniel's mind.

"Well," Daniel says, "I was thinking about telling my nephew to get my musket rifle, but you didn't look so threatening."

"I hope everyone else sees it the same," Colburn says with a small tired smile. "We have strict orders to count everybody, except for the Indians who live on reservations. We started this past August and have nine months to finish recording. And I sure do hope it's not as hot the whole time," Colburn says wiping the sleeve of his shirt across his forehead.

While the men have been talking, people have been gathering off to the side. Daniel's wife is there along with their children, and a collection of neighbors who've come over to collectively make lye soap.

"How often will you be taking this here census?" Daniel asks.

"It will be done every 10 years. Maybe the next time the residents won't be as skeptical." Colburn says hopefully.

"Oh I don't know…. There's something uneasy about strangers coming around asking all kinds of questions," Daniel says with a stern expression on his face.

Colburn nods with understanding. "This will help the state. The count will give us equal representation in Congress so our taxes will be able to help us right here in South Carolina. It will give a somewhat true record of the residents living in America. It will tell us about our young nation. Beg your pardon, but may we trouble you for a drink of water? It's mighty hot."

Daniel calls for Katie, a tall white woman, to bring some water from the well and then asks Colburn, "What do you want to know?"

"First, I have to read this statement to you. *Be it enacted that every person, whose usual place of abode shall be in any family, shall be counted as of such family.* How many people do you have living here, and who is the head of the household?" Colburn asks, beginning to feel as though the long horse ride up the trail might have been worth it after all.

"I'm the head of the household, and there are five people who live here with me. My name is Daniel Eady."

Colburn is reluctant to ask, but knows he has to. "Who is the white lady who brought the water? Is she a slave? It's just that I have yet to see a white lady taking orders from…. Uh, I assume you are a black man?"

"She is my nephew's wife," Daniel responds and then points off towards the shed where a man and woman are watching. "I have two slaves. One is Isaac, and the other is Catherine. They help with the farming and the harvest and go hunting and fishing to provide some of their own meals."

Johnson is clearly agitated by what Daniel is saying, but he doesn't like the way Colburn is talking either. He's never heard a conversation where a white man talks to a black man as an equal. It was true that he'd only been in South Carolina for barely a month, but so far, all the blacks he'd seen were slaves on plantations. They didn't have big plantations where he'd grown up in the North, but his family had owned slaves over many generations. The blacks and whites didn't mingle back home, and from all he'd seen in the south so far, they didn't mingle down here either.

Johnson leans forward in his saddle and interrupts. "I know I'm not from these parts, but this place here is different from what I know, and from what I've seen so far in the South. Are you sayin' you own slaves?" Johnson blurts out, his voice pitching higher with each word. "And who is the Indian lady by the well?"

Daniel stares at Johnson, but his voice is calm and steady. "She's a nearby neighbor, and a friend of my wife. We all live in this area together and help each other out when help is needed. She's here helping to make soap." He turns his gaze back to Colburn. "We've lived here a long time, and this can be a harsh land. So, it doesn't matter what color a person is when they need help."

"Mr. Colburn," Johnson's screechy voice protests, "This is not information that should be on the federal census! We need to go."

"Hold on Johnson," Colburn says matching Daniel's calm tone. "We took an oath to record and count all inhabitants accurately. Besides, there's a column for *all other free persons.* Don't forget, we get paid for the number of people we count."

"Yeah...," Johnson protests weakly, "but I never thought I'd see any Negroes except on the plantations.... It just ain't right!" And with that, Johnson turns his horse, gives it a kick, and runs away down the trail towards the woods.

Colburn looks after the dust that's rising on the trail and sighs. He finishes making his marks in the census book and gives Daniel a quick nod before turning his own horse and heading back down the trail.

Once he was out of sight from the house, Johnson stops and waits for Colburn. When their horses are once again walking back towards the main trail, Johnson breaks the silence. "A Negro owning land and slaves.... I sure do hope we won't be coming across another place like that."

"We don't know what's out here in these woods," Colburn said. "Counting all the inhabitants of this state

has never been done before. This is an historical task that we're a part of, and I'm sure when all is accounted for, we'll see some startling facts about the people of America."

Virginia DeMarce in her essay, Verry Slitly Mixt, states:

Mixed –blood families sometimes lived in the same locations as they have since the 1790 census, and their surname pattern often remained the same.

One anthropologist has noted that as far back as the 1790 census, "the ancestors of these [East Coast] groups seem to have been living in the same locations as we find them today and were classified as mixed-bloods then also. The family names of the groups in 1790 were practically the same as they are today. This was true for those people who stayed in the 1790 settlements locations; the family-name patterns remained stable.

On the following page is the first census of St. Johns Parish, South Carolina, it was enumerated by Colburn. In 1790 he listed George, William, Daniel, Jas. (James) and John Edey as "All other free persons. The term, "All other free persons" refer to non–white inhabitants, it varied what the census enumerator wrote, some wrote Negro, Colored or F.N. for free Negro, F of C for free person of color, F.M.C. for free man of color, F.W.C. for free woman of color, or fb. and fbk. for free black.

An amount of the number of inhabitants of the [illegible] at [illegible]

names of heads of families	Free White males of 16 years and upwards including heads of families	Free white males under 16 years of age	Free white females including heads of families	All other free persons	Slaves
Cox [illegible] Mottrey	1	1	1		127
Rachall Caw	1		1		113
Rachuel Edwards	1		2		75
Honory Caveaner	4				298
William Doisty	2	3	5		[illegible]
Jas. Edison	1		3		18
Daniel Parker				1	1
Francis Parker				1	
[illegible]				3	1
George Eday				6	
William Eday					
Daniel Eday				4	1
Jas. Eday				1	
[illegible] Davis				1	
[illegible] Eday				3	
Jack				3	
William [illegible]				7	
H. William [illegible]				7	
ned tanner				3	3
[illegible]				1	
quack				1	1
[illegible] Williamson	10	4	12	55	717
Jno. Cartall	2	1	6	[illegible]	40
	12	5	18	55	757
am.t of page no. 1	42	25	56		1619
no. 2	43	23	46	5	879
no. 3	35	29	60		747
no. 4	42	45	69		156
no. 5	35	25	76		1012
	209	152	331	60	5170

600

60
331
152
209

Total 5922

Source: South Caroline Department of Archives and History.

The 1800 S.C. Census records show the following living in Charleston District with no white person in the household.

Daniel Eady	*3 Free Persons/ 1 slave*
George Eady	*3 Free Persons*
James Eady	*4 Free Persons*
John Eady	*5 Free Persons*
Jonathan Eady	*9 Free Persons*
William Eady	*9 Free Persons*

Source: Theresa Hicks author of, "South Carolina Indians, Indian Traders and other ethnic connections in 1670."

Chapter 3

Others in the South

A few months following the second census in 1800, Charleston's legislators meet to discuss an increasing problem, they see the number of free blacks has grown on the census. They find colonial laws in the books; however, none address the rights or limitations of free blacks.

They sit around a large table, along the width of the table are lamps casting shadows. The kerosene smell mixes with the cigar smoke like an ambiance of having a problem and not knowing how to solve it.

Abram, the owner of a large plantation sits at the head of the table. He is a heavy man, nearly 60 years old, his eyes gleams in the lamplight. Several petitions lay on the table, from citizens looking to their new government for help with the rising number of free blacks in their city.

"Gentlemen, we continue to see an increasing number of free Negroes in our city," Abram begins, and then stops to draw heavily on his cigar as if to give his comrades time to let the weight of the problem settle. "As you know, their numbers are increasing for various reasons…. Abolitionists continue to send anti-slavery mail antagonizing slave owners. Northerners are sending ministers to our churches to preach against our traditions and way of life, causing many to free their slaves in their last wills and testaments. Others are working and purchasing themselves and family members out of bondage. We also have many who were freed after the Revolutionary War, because of their services."

"Moreover, we have white indentured servants working side-by-side with slaves, who are sleeping with them and having children. As y'all know, the increase is causing great uneasiness among our white citizens. My wife has become very afraid…. She barely sleeps at night. They have also been caught voting in our elections."

> *…beg leave to add to the bad votes mentioned in his memorial the name of (Edwonston?) a free person of color, whose caste has come to the knowledge of your memorialist since the election.*

Source: South Carolina Department of Archives and History.

In 1812 citizens wrote a petition to propose a law to make it illegal for free blacks and slaves to sleep with white women.

> The Honorable the President and Members of the Senate of the State of South Carolina new in Session in Columbia.
>
> The Petition of the Subscribers humbly sheweth (show).
>
> .... attempting to exercise among some of the lower classes of white people freedom and familiarities which are degrading to them and dangerous to society, we allude to attempts which are made and some of them with success at sexual intercourse with white females: an offense to which our existing laws annex no adequate punishment... The want of adequate penalty for such an offense has in some instances induced an...indignant neighbourhood... The necessity of such an resort ought in our opinion of your petitioners to be guarded again by the passage of a law annexing to such criminal conduct a penalty commensurate to the offenses.

Source: South Carolina Department of Archives and History.

Johnson adds, "We also have an influx of black indentured servants from Virginia who have reached the end of their servitude and are moving here, several with their white wives."

Abram continues, his concern resounding through his voice as he reads the petition aloud.

"Now, they are competing with our good white citizens for jobs."

The South Carolina Mechanics Association of carpenters and bricklayers petitioned the courts to be able to compete with the low prices free blacks were charging for their services.

> *To the Honorable the Senate and House of Representatives in General Assembly.*
>
> *The humble Petition of the South Carolina Mechanics Association.*
>
> *…your petitioners would further request that your Honorable body would take with consideration the class of negroes known amongst us as free negroes and that a tax be imposed upon them or that some remedy be made that shall at least place us in such a position that we may be able to compete with them, if they are to be on an equality with us. And your petitioners will ever pray and so forth.*

Source: South Carolina Department of Archives and History.

> *The Petition of the House of Carpenters and Bricklayers in Charlestown*
>
> *Humbly Sheweth(show),*
>
> *That your Petitioners have labored under great inconveniences in their respective occupation…having scarce had sufficient employment to support their families…they apprehend in great measure to a number of…Negro tradesman, who undervalue work. By undertaking it for very little more than the materials would cost, by which it is evident the stuff they work with cannot be honestly acquired. Your Honorable House…this practice must be…not only to the proprietors of materials for building, but highly detrimental to your Petitioners, who are thereby deprived of the means of gaining a livelihood by their industry.*
>
> *Your Petitioners therefore humbly request your Honorable House to take their …case into your serious consideration, and to enact such a law as may prohibit Negroes from undertaking work on their own account, and to adopt such …measures for the redress of said grievance, and for the encouragement of industry as your wisdom shall same meet, and your Petitioners as in duty bound shall pray…*

Source: South Carolina Department of Archives and History.

Johnson listens while Abram reads the petition. He's frowning, and his head is moving from side to side. When Abram finishes, Johnson looks up.

"I was a census marshal for the first census and met a land-owner who was a free black man. When I was leaving, he commanded his dog to chase me!" Johnson knew it was a lie, but the dog had barked, and he was willing to say what he had to. Something had to be done, and some of the men in this room needed to be agitated.

"Some of them are better off than the whites in this city! I see them whenever I go downtown. They own barbershops, and are tailors, dressmakers, and carpenters, while some of our white citizens live destitute lives seeking help from benevolent societies. This problem will continue to increase until we, the good people treat it as a detriment to our city. Lest we fall asleep as if we don't see what's happening."

The men start to discuss the idea of increasing the capitation tax-free blacks already must pay. They adjourn before deciding.

Two months later, they are again in the same room to discuss ways to protect their southernly ways. Sunlight shimmers through a paned window creating a checkered pattern that moves across the floor.

Abram's voice filled with doubt. "Although we are here to consider enacting a law to further tax them, we should consider other means of preventing them from finding ways to be a nuisance."

Johnson interrupts, "we should enact a law to require slave owners to have legislative permission before emancipating slaves. Another problem is some owners allow their slaves to hire themselves out! It's profitable for their masters, but evil to our community. The slaves get a feeling of being almost free," added Johnson.

State of South Carolina Richland District

To the Honorable the President and Members of the Senate.

We have long viewed with great interest and concern, the serious and alarming arising from owners permitting their slaves to hire their own time, upon the payment of certain wages. The demoralizing effects which such a practice is calculated to produce, is daily manifested by the dissolute lives of slaves who are thus licensed, and the baneful influence of their example on the conduct of others. In a prominent degree is this evil exhibited among that class of slaves, who have been trained and instructed in the various mechanical professions. They are enabled to labor at cheaper rates than the free white population of the same employments and thus monopolize, in a great measure, the different mechanical trades; too frequently at the expense and sacrifice of the industrious white mechanics, whose only means of subsistence, and perhaps of a numerous family, alone depends upon his exertions. We cannot but believe, also, that the vital interest of the whole community is materially interested and concerned and eminently endangered by the pursuit and in the continuance of this alarming practice, as has been palpably manifested by the recent and serious occurrences in the city of Charleston, in which the principal plot and scheme originated and was matured by the machination of this very class of our black population.

We, therefore, your petitioners, do earnestly pray, that your Honorable body will enact such laws or legislative provisions, as will immediately and effectually suppress this dangerous and growing practice, and as in duty bound we will ever pray.

Source: South Carolina Department of Archives and History.

Phillip, who has been on the committee for several years, has a lawyer for an uncle, "We must write laws to limit their rights."

Abram raises his fist and slams it down. "More taxes! There's nothing in the laws about how much we can tax. I say we tax them out of this state. Let some other state deal with them."

Phillip hoists his chair forward. "I say we double the tax from two to four dollars."

Johnson speaks up. "The problem is that some of them have been here for generations… some before the city was founded in 1683. They aren't going to leave just because of more taxes. It may cause them hardship, but I doubt they would leave their family members."

"We'll just have to see how much they can endure," Phillip adds with an impassive shrug. "Maybe when they don't have anything to eat, they'll remember how good slavery is, having food to eat and no taxes to pay."

Connor adds, speaking up for the first time. He understands their concerns, and of the people writing petitions, yet he believes in equality. He is on this committee to do what he can on behalf of free blacks and the destitute, which means he must always choose his words carefully. He is not convinced that another tax is the best course of action. ""We should consider the flag is to protect the person of everyone it covers, an increase in the tax would impose a great hardship for our women citizens."

A petition was written by free men of color who did not want the two-dollar capitation tax to apply to women without a husband or a father.

To the Honorable the Senate and House of Representative of the state aforesaid.

The petition of the undersign sheweth (show) That a poll tax of two dollars a head is imposed by law upon the free coloured population of this state, that this tax though small bears with great severity upon the female part of the class of people alluded to, especially when unprotected by husband or father who could provide for them. They are generally persons in extremely destitute circumstances, and by law are subject to be sold if unable to pay the tax. Your petitioners respectfully pray that the law may be repealed, and that helpless females may not be sold on account of their poverty.

Source: South Carolina Department of Archives and History.

Abram's brows gully and he taps his chin while he disregards Connor's response. "The original law imposed a two-dollar tax to be paid by all free blacks annually in 1792, although we haven't been as strict as we should have been with collecting it. We can impose a penalty to be arrested on those who don't pay and give the sheriffs an added incentive by taking it out of their budgets if they fail to collect," Abrams adds, self-assured with his solution. "We have another option; Phillip's uncle has found a way for us to put them in a Workhouse."

> *To Nathaniel G. Cleary Esquire, Sheriff of Charleston District or to his lawful deputy.*
>
> *...of the said several free negroes... The said sum of two-dollars each together with the lawful charged ...and in case the said...refuse or neglect to produce goods and chattels sufficient to...that then you take the body of each...and convey them, him or her to the Common Goal or Workhouse commanding the keeper of the said Goal or Workhouse to retain the body or bodies of the said...in his custody until he, she, or they pay the sum of two dollars each, together with the charge of keeping detaining as a foresaid and for your so doing this shall be your sufficient warrant- given under my hand of seal at this general tax office in Charleston...*
>
> *Sam Buger*

Source: South Carolina Department of Archives and History.

Free blacks did not want to pay the higher taxes imposed on them. They continue to feel the pressure of the laws determined to limit their rights, to know their whereabouts, and to levy taxes on them.

But instead of giving up and leaving South Carolina, they take their cases to court.

"What if someone has Indian blood?" Connor asks with hesitation.

"The Indians aren't liable to pay the capitation taxes," Abram states grimly. "But if someone tries to get out of the tax by claiming they're Indian, they'll need to go to court with a legal affidavit to confirm it. It's time to increase our collecting efforts and show them that times are changing."

The number of free blacks arrested increased significantly once the legislative committee began to strictly enforce the payments of capitation taxes. Nevertheless, free blacks were not the only people who felt the effects of these taxes, sheriffs and tax collectors felt some uneasiness.

To the honorable President and members of the Senate.

The humble petition of David Becket late Sheriff of Richland District. Respectfully sheweth. That the tax collector for Richland District lodged a number of executions in his hands for collection, against Free people of Colour, amounting to two hundred and sixty three dollars for which the Treasurer now holds his receipts. That the time allowed by law for the return of these executions is too short, and that the difficulty of finding them, on account of the peculiar situation of their place of residence, is such that it was impossible for the Sheriff to collect the above amount. He therefore prays this honorable body to release him from the payment of the said two hundred and sixty three dollars, and he will ever pray.

Source: South Carolina Department of Archives and History.

The tightening of the law causes many free blacks to go to court to prove their Indian ancestry, so they wouldn't have to deal with the uncertainty of being arrested.

Three months later in a windowless courtroom, a wave of suspense spreads across a hearing in St. Johns Parish.

The parish is amid a drought. The ground is parching, and the soil is beginning to shatter like broken hopes. To shun the heat, they make fans with sticks and cardboards. The long wait is causing them to be restless about the upcoming ruling.

Abruptly the back door opens with a squeak and a tall slim man wearing a suit and white shirt appears, his silky black tie is tied loosely at the neck. He twists his pencil thin mustache and quickly walks to the front of the courtroom. He has put lots of consideration in his clothes today, knowing the Charleston Mercury

newspaper would be present. The Weston brothers, two of Charleston's most successful black tailors, made his suit.

He shouts with a clear semi-baritone voice as if he is reciting literature by Shakespeare. "Everyone in court stand for the entering of the Honorable Judge Henry."

Everyone stood to watch the judge enter. They are all here for the same reason. In the silence, their fans shift from side-to-side in poetic togetherness.

Judge Henry, a rugged man, enters and gradually walks to his seat behind the bench, faintly gasping for air by the end of the short trip. He is struggling with the dry heat, for he'd recently moved from up north.

He slowly looks across the room from left to right, not expecting to see it almost filled with blacks.

The bailiff, sounding as chipper as a blue bird in a dogwood tree, makes a gaudy shout, "Everyone be seated and get ready to hear from the Honorable Judge Henry."

A half-smoked cigar drapes from the side of the judge's mouth, it's held firmly in place by habit as he begins speaking. "So, you are telling me that many of the colored population of this parish have Indian blood."

The judge removes his cigar and looks around the room. There isn't an empty seat. "I imagine these cases are somehow related to blacks being exempt from the capitation tax?" Well… let's get on with it. I want to be finished with all these cases by noon. I have some fishing to do."

"I don't suppose these cases are in some type of order?"

The Negro law of South Carolina collected and digested by John Belton O' Neall, 1848, Section 53, suggest a law that allows free blacks to petition the court on legal matters.

Free negroes, mulattoes.... may make all necessary affidavits on collateral matters, in cases in the Superior Courts, in which they may be parties....

Jim shuffles the paperwork, hurrying to answer. "Yes Sir. These three ladies are first."

"Okay ladies… step forth," the judge says, his hastiness fades as he admires their caramel-colored skin.

The women politely approach the judge, stopping behind a table positioned in front of the judge's bench. All wearing their Sunday dresses, hoping to make a good impression. They're desperately hoping for a good outcome.

"Why are you here in court today?" the judge asks.

Polly Eady, the eldest of the three at 35-years-old, speaks. "To prove our Indian ancestry."

The judge maintains a distant expression while being gripped by their beauty. While living in the north, he'd had several affairs with women from the court room. Clearing his throat, he announces, "Although you ladies appear to be of mixed ancestry, both the law and the judicial system require written evidence that legally proves your Indian Ancestry."

"Yes Sir. We are here to submit our proof," Polly replies, her nerves causing her voice to shake. "I have an affidavit from my neighbor saying we are mixed blood Indians."

"What does it say?" the judge asks, looking for the opportunity to help the women… and possibly enjoy the benefits of his kindness.

Holding the document in her quivering hands she reads, her voice starting to vibrate like an un-tuned violin. "This is to certify Polly, Nancy, and Patty Edy was born of Indian descent. They are from the same family as John Edy."

"Jim," The judge demands. "Pass that over to me so I can take an accurate look."

S.C. Marion Dist. This is to certify Polly, Nancy [or?] Patty Edy was free born of the Indian descent. They are the same family as John Edy. 29 Mar. 1826. S / Joseph Davis. At the request of Ann Edy and Martha Curtis, two free women of colour and both of them daughters of Molly Edy, I do certify that I have known them all for a very long time.

Source: South Carolina Indians, Indian Traders and other ethnic connections, in 1670, by Theresa Hicks.

Free African Americans in Virginia, North Carolina and South Carolina, by Paul Heinegg, further states the status of John, Molly and Nancy as "Other Free":

John, head of a St. John's Parish, Charleston household of 1 "other free" in 1790 and 5 "other free" in 1800. He paid tax on 1 "free Black" in Prince George Parish, South Carolina, in 1825.

Molly, head of a Liberty County household of 6 "other free" in 1800.

Nancy, head of a Liberty County household of 7 "other free" in 1800.

The judge takes a few minutes to look the papers over – an eternity for the women. "Jim, let there be a written document to show that these ladies are exempt from having to pay the capitation tax." He turns to the women with a content expression, "You ladies may leave. Have a pleasant day." Then he turns to Jim. "Who do we have next?" he demands.

"Sir, we have Laura Breach of Charleston."

The judge eyes her over as she approaches. "From your looks, you are here because of the same tax?"

"Yes Sir. I wish to avoid paying this tax, I have a statement from Samuel Foxworth declaring that I am of

Indian descent," Laura says, feeling more poised after hearing the judge's first decision.

The judge raises his eyebrows. "Read it aloud for the court to hear," he says with a sigh.

> *"This is to declare that Laura Breach is the Granddaughter of George Eady, who was in all cases recognized as an Indian, and who did marry a white woman, Rachel Brown,"*
>
> *Source of the above affidavit: South Carolina Indians, Indian Traders and other ethnic connections in 1670, by Theresa Hicks.*

"Bring the affidavit here Jim," the judge says holding his hand out to receive it. A look of scrutiny on his face. "Okay, that's enough evidence for the court. Step to the side and you'll get your exemption papers. Jim, bring me the next case," the judge says as he looks across the room.

The judge looks at the next person and asks the same question, "Why are you in court today?"

"I am here to be exempt from having to pay this tax, which would cause hardship for me and my family," Hester Blute says, a hint of hope shimmering through her voice.

"Read the affidavit you brought," the judge says, with a sigh.

> *"Indian Sarah, who was married to a white man during the revolutionary war, of which marriage a daughter was born, named Jemima, who intermarried with one Daniel Eady, an Indian by which connexion, they produced Ester Blute.*
>
> *Source: South Carolina Indians and other ethnic connections beginning in 1670, by Theresa Hicks.*

"Who's next?" the judge asks, feeling his fishing time swimming away.

Jim calls two women. The judge looks at them and asks, "Why should you be exempt from the capitation tax?"

Ella, who is standing there with an elderly woman says, "Well sir, Catherine Lands swears that she had known my great-grandmother Shirley, who was married to a white man during the American Revolutionary."

"Is there anyone else who can make a claim on this statement?" the judge asks.

A white man of a respectable stature approaches the judge with the aid of a walking cane. "Judge Honorable, Indian Shirley has always been a respectable inhabitant of this parish. Her claims to *white laws* never called into question until lately after people started going to jail for not paying this tax. She has been brought before this court by the words of some malignantly disposed person who wants her in jail."

"Jim, gather all the affidavits, carefully look over all the details, and bring them to me in my chambers. When you're finished, I'll sign the exemption documents.

At the next meeting, Abrams announces, "I am pleased to say that the increased capitation tax on free blacks has increased our municipal revenues. We now have money we can use to build bridges and develop roads."

Johnson interrupts with clear contempt in his voice. "Maybe so, but many of them escaped the tax by going to court."

Tax returns of free blacks who paid the capitation tax in 1824.

Jonathan Eady of St. Stephens paid a two-dollar free black capitation tax on his tax return in 1824, he owned 4 slaves and 680 acres of land. Source: SC Dept. of Archives and History.

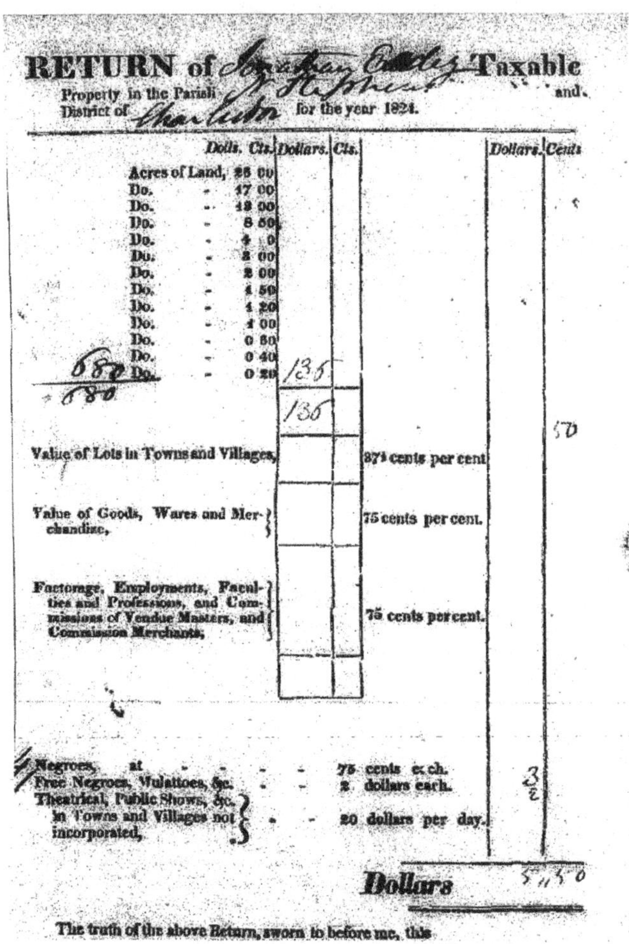

Source: South Carolina Department of Archives and History.

Sarah Eady paid a two-dollar free black capitation tax in Prince George Parish on her tax return in 1824, SC.

Thomas Eady paid a two-dollar free black capitation tax in Prince George Parish on his tax return in 1824.

John Eady paid a two-dollar free black capitation tax in St. John's Parish on his tax return in 1824.

A petition by free blacks, they are required to pay a free black capitation tax and will have to pay the property tax also. They want the capitation tax to be repeal since white citizens aren't paying the tax.

> *State of South Carolina,*
>
> *To the honorable the President and members of the Senate. The petition of whose names are hereunto subscribed sheweth. That by a law of this state we are compelled to pay a tax of two dollars per head in addition to the tax we pay on our property. We beg leave respectfully to state to your honorable house the equity of making a discrimination between free people of color, free negroes possessing taxable property and for free people of color and free negroes not possessing taxable property. Your petitioners who have property, and others who are in the same situation, made by this law to pay a greater tax than any other class of the community. Your petitioners therefore pray that the capitation tax may be repealed, so far as this relates to them who possess property and pay tax there on. Your petitioners will pray so forth.*
>
> *1809*

Source: South Carolina Department of Archives and History.

A petition to impose greater taxes on free persons of color.

> *On the 21ˢᵗ day of December 1822 …an act to establish a competent force to act as a municipal guard for the protection of Charleston and it's vicinity it was enacted that for the purpose of defraying the expenses of the said guard, a tax of ten dollars should be imposed on all houses within the limits of guards or inhabited by negroes or persons of color either as tenant or owners.*

Source: South Carolina Department of Archives and History.

The harsh laws make it difficult for free blacks to maintain a living, causing some to relinquish their free status.

> *To the Honorable the Speaker and other members of the House of Representative.*
>
> *The petition of Daniel Freeman a free person of color...state of South Carolina. Respectfully sheweth (show) unto your honorable body that he is assured that a condition of slavery would be preferable to his present condition as a free person of color. That he is assigning to relinquish his present dubious condition of freedman and to service to himself the benefits of protection and slavery which will arise from the relations of master and servant...upon John B. Morman of the district state aforesaid...*
>
> *his*
> *Daniel X Freeman*
> *mark*

Source: South Carolina Department of Archives and History.

Whites with dark complexions must pay unless they can prove otherwise by petitioning the court. Many free blacks with light skin complexions deny their African heritage to avoid paying the tax.

> *To the Honorable the Senate and House of Representatives of the Legislature of South Carolina.*
>
> *The humble petition of Hiram Floyd of Marion District sheweth(show) unto your Honorable body. That his mother is a free white woman. That his father is also a free man both of rather dark complexion but not so dark as a mulatto and your petitioner is also of a dark complexion which has caused him to be called a free man of color and this induced the tax collector to require him to pay tax as a free person of color. That he refused to pay the tax and that the tax collector caused an execution to be issued against him for the said tax, and being advised to pay the tax he did pay the sum of three dollars and forty cents and cost which with the tax amounted to four dollars 95cents.*

Source: South Carolina Department of Archives and History.

> *To the Honorable the Senate and House of Representative of the State of South Carolina*
>
> *The petitioner of Betty Hunter shewith(show) that she is a mulatto woman, that her mother was a free white woman that has been…taxed as a free negro…*
>
> *York District*

Source: South Carolina Department of Archives and History.

A free man of color is sold into slavery for not paying the capitation tax.

> *To the Honorable the Senate of the State of South Carolina*
>
> *The petition of James Mickenly respectfully sheweth(show) that your petitioner purchased …. a negro man name James Walker…. for arrearage of taxes due this state…. He James Walker having come into the state since the act was passed …. on each free negro per year, that come to reside within the state since the act was passed.*
>
> *At the time your petitioner purchased said Walker an agreement was made between the sheriff….an your petitioner….*

Source: South Carolina Department of Archive and History.

The Act of 1833 directs the issuing of executions against free negroes, mulattoes…who may fail to pay the tax, and that under them, they may be sold for a term, not exceeding one year…The constitutionality of the provision for the sale of free negroes in payment of their taxes is exceedingly questionable.

Source: The Negro law of South Carolina, collected and digested by John Belton O' Neall, 1848, Section 54

Nor has the taxes stop free blacks from continuing to earn enough money to purchase family members away from slavery.

> *The humble petition of Allen Kelly a free man of colour residing in the Villiage of Laurens by trade a blacksmith sheweth(show it) that he purchased in the year 1821 his son George a slave for whom he paid the sum of six hundred and four dollars that your petitioner is desirous of manumitting and setting free his said son George Kelly- your petitioner therefore most humbly pray your Honorable body to take into consideration his petitioner and grant him permission to indulge in so humane and desirable an object in manumitting and setting free his said son...*
>
> *his*
>
> *Witness John Garllington   Signed Allen X Kelly*
>
> *mark*

Source: South Carolina Department of Archives and History.

> *District October Term 1807*
>
> *We present at a great grievance that Negroes are permitted to keep dogs and we recommend to the legislature to pass a law authorizing the patrols to kill any dog which they may find with negroes....*

Source: South Carolina Department of Archives and History.

> *The prayer of your petitioners citizens of Collecton district respectfully sheweth([show] that the law respecting Negroes and free people of colour carring and using firearms not punishable except by forfeiture of said arms, your petitioners think said punishment to light, and think the law ought to be so framed as to make them liable to indictment and punishment on proof that such persons have firearms in their possession whether said arms can be seized or not.*

Source: South Carolina Department of Archives and History.

Chapter 4

Deeper South

On their way home from a trip to the city, William and Daniel decides to take a different route. They'll get home later because of it, this route will take them by the Pendarvis Plantation a free person of color. They'd heard awful things about the plantation, but no one had seen it. Bristow is sitting on the back of the wagon filled with supplies, watching the unfamiliar landscape pass by, wondering why they are taking a different route.

The main crop on the plantation is cotton, as the woods give way to huge fields; they see large groups of slaves on both sides of the road. All of them are working hard to till the soil for cottonseeds.

The treatment of the slaves is harsh. On each side of the road there are men on horseback constantly looking around and demanding them to work harder.

It's late afternoon, that means the slaves have been working in the hot sun for many hours. William and Daniel have worked hard like this, but it was on their own land. The soil they tilled, planted, worked, and harvested fed their own family and made them money. This was different, the sight had them riding past the fields in silence.

This is the first time Bristow has seen slavery on such a large scale. He can hear the slaves singing, it doesn't change the reality of what he's seeing, and he tries to sort it out in his mind. His Uncle Daniel owns three slaves but doesn't treat them anything like this. Isaac, the older of the two male slaves, goes fishing when he has a mind to, Bristow wonders if these slaves get to go fishing.

On Sundays, Bristow sits in church with people who are slaves. He doesn't talk to the adults at church, he talks to their children, and the thought of children and slavery makes him look hard into the field of men trying to gauge how old they are.

The stories of his ancestors and their revolt against the Spaniards come into his mind. Leaving him with a question, "Is this the slavery they fought against. "He could understand fighting against this. He would have fought against it too. In a way, he wanted to fight now. This was wrong.

When their wagon reaches the edge of the woods, Bristow silently hops down, runs to one of the large oak trees on the side of the road. He pulls his hatchet and quickly chops huge markings into the trunk. It wasn't much, but he'd felt compelled to do something. Then, just as quickly and silently, he runs back and hops onto the wagon, listening to the fading sound of the slave's singing as the wagon continues down the road towards home.

The Pendarvis family was one of the largest free colored families in South Carolina to own slaves. James Pendarvis paid taxes on 123 slaves and owned 3,250 acres of land.

James Pendarvis is enumerated on the 1790 census in St. Pauls Parish as, "All other free persons." The last column is the number of slaves he owned.

CHARLESTON DISTRICT, ST. PAULS PARISH.

Pendarvis, James........	1	....	....	1	123
Pendarvis, Will⁺ (Est.).	....	1	1	....	44
Stewart, Ja⁺.........	1	2	3	1	4
Richards, Elizᵗ........	....	....	4	....	23
McLaughling, Jn'o......	1	1	1	....	....

Source: United States Census, 1790.

The chart shows from 1790 to 1860 most free black slave owners live in Charleston compared to other counties in South Carolina. They purchase family members out of slavery and non-family members for benevolence and kindness. In addition to having needs for apprentices in their various trades, barbering, carpentry, bricklaying, bakery, tailoring and other skilled jobs. In rural areas small farmers needed them to maintain the crop. and for a few it was monetary gain.

District	1790	1800	1810	1820	1830	1840	1850	1860
Abbeville					2	7		
Anderson						1	1	1
Barnwell		1		1		5	4	3
Beaufort	2	2	1	4	6			4
Charleston	49	36	17*	206	407	402	266	137
Chesterfield				1	2	1		
Colleton					8	4	2	3
Edgefield			3		1			2
Fairfield								2
Georgetown		2	7	10		13	10	8
Horry							1	
Kershaw			1	2	5			
Lancaster	1					1		
Lauren				1		1		
Lexington								1
Marion		2	2					
Newberry					8	2		2
Orangeburgh	7	1			1	5	2	2
Pendleton				1				
Picken							2	
Richland					7	11	4	1
Sumter		1	1	4	1	1	4	4
Union								1
Williamsburgh					1			
York					1		1	
Total	59	45	32	230	450	454	297	171

Source: Black Slaveowners: Free Black Slave Masters in South Carolina, 1790- 1860, by Larry Koger.

Chapter 5

Shady Streets

It's an early Saturday afternoon on a cloudy day in downtown Charleston. The tree sheltered streets are busy with people walking along rugged sidewalks, as riders maneuver their horses around slow-moving buggies. The light autumn wind is warm; it carries sounds of good conversations and laughter along its currents.

Polly pulls her buggy to a stop near the general store, she'd just left the bank. She dreads going to the bank because the money is printed with images of slaves. She opposes her uncle owning slaves and does what she can to feed runaways seeking refuge at their settlement. She and her sister Nicole step down, smoothing out their fine skirts, ready to enjoy a pleasant afternoon.

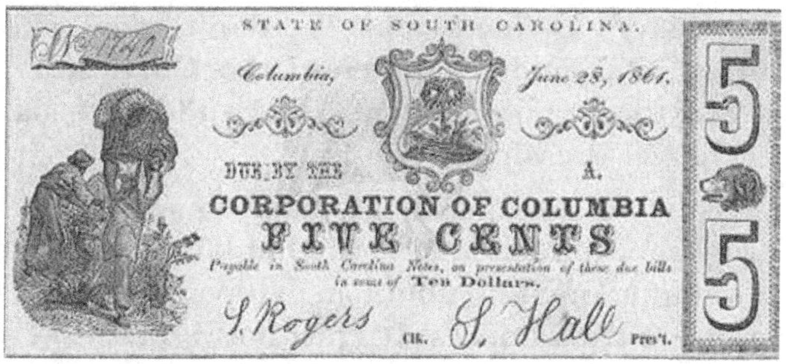

Source: John W. Jones, The Color of Money exhibit, he discovered depictions of slaves on money in the south.

Their first stop is Julie's general store where they do their weekly shopping. A small group of white men are sitting on a bench in front of the store, watching the people pass by. This includes Polly and Nicole as they walk by on their way into the store.

Johnson, whose face has creased and furrowed with age, is standing in front of the store across the street. He frowns at the two women walking into the store, telling his wife there should be laws against them walking on our sidewalks.

His wife Henrietta follows his stare and squabbles, "Everywhere I look anymore, them folks are prancing around our streets."

Johnson's feelings are evident in his tone, "We're working on laws for them, so they will know their place." Over the years, Johnson has told anyone who would listen to the story of Daniel commanding his dog on him, each telling further fueling his dislike towards all free blacks in the city.

Henrietta vigorously adds her two cents. "I've been hearing stories of slaves who walk around passing themselves as free blacks. We don't know who is who anymore! I wrote a letter to the Charleston Gazette telling them about how free blacks and town slaves have been over-dressing in the city."

Johnson smacks his hand in agreement. "A few of us sent official letters of complaint about the sheriff not doing anything about an extravagant entertainment at one of their houses. It's just not right."

State of South Carolina

City of Charleston…

…at the house…saw a number of people of color collected in and about said house, that their appearance of being noisy and riotous, drew attention. That they looked into the said house and saw a table of bread with a vanity of delicacies, served on China. The center of the table decorated with a pyramid and large icing cake, that shortly after they saw…Moses, who after some conversation with a Negro fellow…entered the house and brought out several of the articles purposed for the …entertainment and left them on the ground for the neighbors about to behold the extravagance, Captain Cunnington (sheriff) then came up and asked Mr. Moses by what authority he dared enter that house calling him a house robber or words to that effect and making use of such other abusive language, that Johnson…told Mr. Cunnington he was astonished at such language from a magistrate…further say that Mr. Cunnington laid hold of said Moses and pushed him out of said house with violence.

William Johnson

J. Alyson

Source: South Carolina Department of Archives and History.

A bell rings as Polly and Nicole walk through the front door. The store is immaculate, aisles of hardwood floors are polished clean. One aisle is filled with a variety of dishes, including fine porcelain cups and saucers, another is filled with canned goods and general household supplies. At the front of each aisle, by the front windows, are baskets of sweet Carolina peaches. At the back of the store, there are barrels filled with flour, corn meal, rice, and sugar.

Julie, the owner of the store, is a friendly white woman in her mid-60s. She is wearing a bright floral dress and sitting on a stool behind the counter reading the newspaper. When the sisters come in, she puts the paper down and greets them. "Howdy."

"Howdy Missus. Julie," they both respond with a smile.

"Those are lovely skirts," Mrs. Julie says. "Is this your work Nicole? I remember you saying you were taking up sewing."

Nicole smiles, but its Polly who speaks up. "Yes. She has picked it up and taken to it quickly! She made these and has spruced up most of our others." Polly embarrassed by her bragging lowers her head. "I know it might be a bit of showin' off to wear them on a Saturday, but we can't wear them on the farm."

Julie looks down at the work dress she's wearing and shrugs. "I don't dare wear my nice dresses to work. You know, I was just reading a letter in the newspaper. It's another complaint about free blacks over-dressing in the city."

Nicole shakes her head. "We've heard about letters like that, you know how folks can be. It just seems vain that dresses – could ruffle so many feathers."

Julie declares, "You know, it seems like they're always trying to harass y'all. What gets me is all this dreadful talk about passing a law that would put free black folks into slavery." Julie sees the looks on the women's face and wishes she hadn't said it. "But you know what," she says, trying to recover, "They hardly follow through much anyways, and y'all are some kind of Indian. Any ways, never mind my rambling. What can I get for you ladies today?"

Polly has never been one to run away from the truth. "You're a kind lady Mrs. Julie, and we hope they don't follow through."

Johnson hasn't moved. He's been watching the women through the store windows and just knew they were bragging about their clothing. The same group of white men are still sitting on the bench. Johnson makes his decision, tells Henrietta to stay put, and heads across the street.

The group of men are enjoying their usual Saturday afternoon company, watching people while talking about their crops, and whatever else is of interest. Johnson signals his greetings and leans against the wall, adding bits to the conversation when he can. As he stands there, a well-dressed black man rides by on a horse.

Johnson turns his head, he doesn't accept any of them having more than whites, "I have had it! What about those two in the store? It just ain't right, dressing like they're better off than my wife."

The men look at Johnson. Julie's husband Robert is sitting with them. The man sitting on Robert's left is a white man who lives with a black woman. They've all been neighbors for many years.

Robert has heard talk like this before. He's seen and read the petitions – including the one written about him. But like many people, he's learned to choose his battles. As he looks at the man leaning against the wall of his store, he recognizes who he is—Johnson.

A petition to prohibit white men from living openly with Negro and mulatto women. A copy of the original petition is on the following page.

To the Honorable the members of the members of the Senate and House of Representative of the Legislator of South Carolina. We the undersigned citizens of the state of South Carolina, humbly petition your honorable to take into consideration the fact that white men in this community are frequently found living in open connections with negro and mulatto women, in a manner in reputable to the neighborhood...setting a pernicious example to our youngster, and .... the institution of slavery...therefore...to your honorable.... that you make it by enactment at this session of the legislature and indictable offense for any white man, resident in this state, to live in open connection with a negro or mulatto woman as his wife, whether married or unmarried.

Source: South Carolina Department of Archives and History.

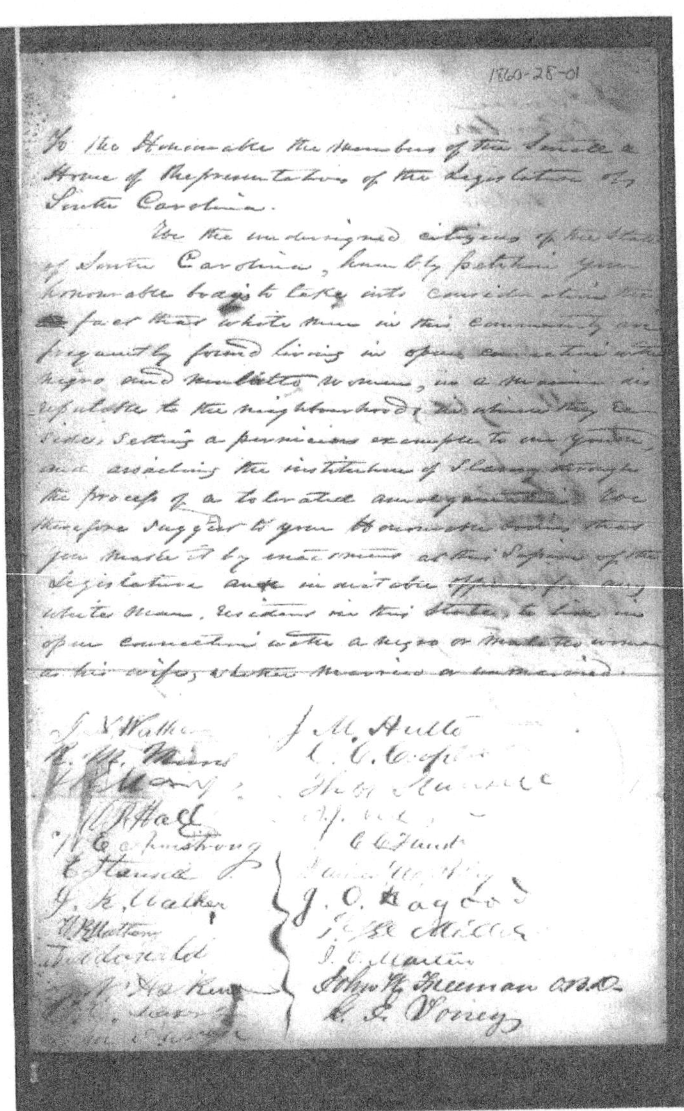

Source: South Carolina Department of Archives and History.

The will of Isaac Bourdeaux, a white man who lived with a black woman and her children. The term "issue" meant mixed in South Carolina during this time.

> ···In Trust to and for the use benefit and behalf of Martha Chaves, a free young black Woman residing with me, and her issue (children)···. I give and bequeath to the Said Martha Chaves two hundred and fifty dollars annually···I give and bequeath to the said Martha Chaves, all my cattle, including cows, calves and also my horse called Puney also all and singular the articles of my household and kitchen furniture···. June 12th 1820.

Source: South Carolina Department of Archives and History.

"They are respectable people not causing any more trouble than the unruly whites as far as I can see. They make a living and pay their taxes, even more taxes than we do. Some are shiftless and cause unrest, but so do some of us. The only time there's trouble is when the whites decide it's time to pass another law to put more hardship on them. They come into my store and many of the other shops around here. We know them. They stop by my house for visits. Occasionally, we even have supper together."

Johnson responds, "It's not right that they should have more than us whites, y'all see them riding full speed on their horses through our city like they own it!"

Source: South Carolina Department of Archives and History.

> *.... slaves and free people of colour riding horses at full speed in the publick streets especially on Sabbath days....*

"Some of us are having trouble just buying seeds for our harvest. They should be picking my cotton. My brother went out of business because of black farmers selling low price vegetables."

Robert knows full well that you can't argue the ignorance out of anybody, and he's had enough of the charade. "Johnson," he interrupts, "You ain't got no cotton."

Johnson continues, not caring that he's been exposed. "I don't know how it got this way, but we're going to change it. We're going to put a stop to all of it!"

Polly and Nicole drive their buggy down a series of Charleston's streets based on a map drawn by Bristow. Next to the courthouse, they see a building construction.

They are amazed at the intricate work being done on the Iron Gate and talk about how years ago most of the white workers were hired to do the "skilled" work. Now, an increasing number of free blacks are skilled laborers and artisans. They were willing to work for lower wages than their white competition.

A growing population of German indentured servants are reaching the end of their service terms and immigrating to Charleston. They compete for the same jobs as free blacks and are willing to charge even lower prices, this has increased the number of petitions against free blacks carrying on a trade.

Petition of the Mechanics, Artisans and others of the City of Charleston, praying the enactment of a law to prevent free Negroes or persons of color from carrying on any trade, calling or occupation in their own name or the name of others.

Source: South Carolina Department of Archives and History.

As Polly and Nicole neared their destination, they slowed down along a stretch of row houses in Charleston's 6th Ward. It is warm, and many people were sitting on their porches, talking, and carrying on with daily routines. Two teenagers holding hands and giggling ran across the street in front of the buggy.

Once, this had been a community occupied only by free blacks. Now, German and Irish immigrants had settled here. Town slaves lived here too, working and taking their wages to their masters. Masters who didn't trust their town slaves were paid directly.

Polly finally pulls the buggy to a stop and the sisters eagerly walk towards the front door of the last house in the row. A street sign confirms that they are on Wentworth Street.

Researchers at The Charleston Museum prepared this map to show were concentrated areas of free blacks lived in Charleston.

Ann Eady, living on Wentworth Street in Charleston about 1811-1817 when she paid the "free Negro" capitation tax [Capitation Tax Book, p.5].

Source: Free African Americans of NC, VA and SC, by Paul Heinegg.

Polly lightly knocks on the door. There isn't an immediate answer, the sisters share a disappointing look, hoping not to have made the trip in vain.

The door slowly opens and their sister Ann, wiping her hands on a long blue-floral apron, takes the sight of her sisters in. It's been a long while since they've been together, and she's thrilled at the sight of them on her doorstep. A warm smile graces her pecan-brown face as she hugs her sisters then rushes them into the sitting room.

"It's so good to see y'all! I fancy the letters, but this is so much better. Sit and you can tell me everything. How is life on the settlement?

"It's the same; we can catch up on that. How's Caleb?"

Ann blushes. "He's fine." Caleb is a town slave. There are about twice as many free black women in the city than free black men. So, the women often marry town slaves. The two have been married just short of a year, and this is the first time she's seen her sisters since the wedding. "He'll be here before the 9 o'clock slave curfew. When he gets here, he'll secure the buggy for the night."

A rapid knock sounds from the front door. Ann answers it and sees Maggie, a blue-eyed little girl, standing on the stoop. She's wearing a bright yellow handmade dress, and has a tin cup cuddled between her small hands.

"Mama says to ask if you got some suhca?" Maggie asks, her Irish and southern accents melding together.

"Sure darling. Wait right here and I'll get it for you." Ann takes the cup into the kitchen and comes back with it filled. She carefully puts the cup of sugar in Maggie's hands and looks at her with a serious expression. "Careful not to spill… and tell your Mama I said for her to stop by when she can."

"Yes, Ma'am," Maggie says before turning and skipping her way down the front steps.

Ann looks after the little girl as she crosses the street. The sun is sinking now. Inside the small row house, the aroma of the one-pot meal fills the room.

"Y'all must be hungry for supper considering all the traveling you've done," Ann says. "I've made plenty."

Polly and Nicole smooth their skirts out as they stand. "Oh my," Ann says. "Your skirts are beautiful. Things must be going well."

As the women move into the kitchen and start setting the table, the conversation begins to flow as easily as it ever has. "Things are about the same," Polly starts. "It's Nicole. She's taken up sewing."

"It was your letters that got me thinking about it," Nicole says. "You told me that you liked being a seamstress, and that there was plenty of work if you were good at it. Every bit helps."

Ann grinned. "I was fortunate to find someone to apprentice with. She's a nice white lady who's taught lots of women. She even helped me get a job in a dress shop."

"One of the ladies from church took me on. She doesn't do much fancy stuff, but I'd learned enough to make some things," Nicole says while she does a slow twirl so her sister can get a good look. "How is it working in a dress shop?" she asks, wanting to hear all the details of a "city" job.

"It's good…. It's just that it isn't always what you'd expect. I have to be perfect with every stitch. If I'm not, someone else will get my job for sure. Maggie's mom is a seamstress she works on lace. She learned how to make lace from her momma before she came over.

But there are a lot of Irish women who do lace-work, so there's a lot of competition for those jobs."

"I don't know if I'm ready to get a job yet," Nicole says, "But it's nice to think about."

A blurry sunshine warms William Eady as he hitches his horse. A post office made of course red bricks has "Post Office" hand-painted on a sign above the building's entrance.

A small room is occupied by a woman, she knows almost everybody's business and often likes to share it. She is older, tannish white and wearing rounded glasses. She walks away from sorting the mail as soon as she sees William. He knows her because she's worked in this office for at least as long as he's been coming here to collect his mail.

William watches her move to the area where the mail is stored. The loosely organized mail covers a few tables. She looks through a stack, pulls out a collection of letters, and walks back to her window.

She smiles at William almost apologetically, motioning to the stacks of mail behind her. "I haven't finished sorting all of this mail out yet. It's been a busy month, with all the letter writing going on. Seems like there are plenty of folks writing to newspapers after the Demark Vesey conspiracy," she says, passing the letter to William. "This is all your mail," she adds. "There's even been talk of stopping free blacks from receiving mail."

William surveys the letter in his hand with a concerned look on his face. "I don't know what my mail's going to say. I've heard about people getting letters saying they aren't legally free," he says, his thumb grazing over the name on the top letter of the stack. It's his name, but he won't open it here. "Thank you, ma'am, and have a good day," he says with a polite wave before turning and leaving.

The woman looks at him through the large front window, hoping she didn't just hand him a letter that would tell him he wasn't legally free.

On a mid-September afternoon, the Cumbos and Locklears families have gathered at the Eady settlement to celebrate. It's been a good year for their crops, and with most of it harvested, everyone has a reason to celebrate. The men have gathered to talk business and are hoping William doesn't drink too much as he often does on these occasions. They are sitting on wooden chairs and stumps while taking turns roasting a pig on an outdoor fire.

Daniel and his son Daniel P. had gotten up very early that day to get the fire going. The pig was seasoned the night before and kept on a block of ice, until the starter woods were hot enough for roasting. Families have brought squirrels and rabbits to add to the day's feast, but it's the aroma of the roasted pork that filled the air.

The women were busy setting up tables placed beneath the bows of a large shade tree. They set down plates and eat-ware and placed the collection of cooked and fresh vegetables dishes along the length of the tables, chatting while keeping an easy eye on the dozen or so children running around the yard.

As their shared feast was about to begin, William Eady stood to say a few words. "This is a good day with friends and family."

William pauses, but everyone knows this is his way. He always has more to say, and in the silence, he's created, everyone hears the sounds of the farm around them – the cattle moving around, horses swishing water in the trough, and chickens clucking as they hunt down their afternoon meal. "It's a good day to give thanks for all that we have."

"Amen!" Bristow Jr. says while raising his glass of sugar water. He knew it might not have been good manners to say something before his Grandfather was done talking, but his Grandfather was known to go on and on, and he was hungry. This was going to be his last year at the children's table – one last chance to get away with something.

William turned to the children's table with a raised brow and waited a few more seconds before breaking into a smile. "Amen," he said.

When dinner was over, people found seats around the fire. Once again, William stood, this time surveying the group of people who had gathered. He knows all of them, right down to the youngest, and he understands the importance of gatherings like this because there's more to it than sharing food. These are people who do what they can to help each other. The low country is not always generous to the people who work the land. There are hard times, and during those times, its family, neighbors, and friends you can count on who might make the difference between freedom and slavery.

"We have lived on this land for many generations," he starts. "It feels good knowing that by the grace of God, we have been able to make it through the struggles we've had to face. Our children are free. They use that freedom to run and play, soon enough, they will each be doing their part to preserve the freedoms and the land our ancestors fought for."

William looks over to Bristow Jr. "Why look at little Bristow. It seems like it was only yesterday I was teaching him how to hunt squirrels. He's practically a grown man."

Bristow holds his chin up at his grandfather's words, his hand falling to the hatchet hanging from his side.

"These are hard times," William continues. "We all know people who have lost their freedom or left because they feared losing their freedom. We will not leave. Our people fought for this land, and we will continue to do what we need to do to make sure that we, and our land, stay free."

They were stirring words, but they were challenging words. Polly has heard her uncle speak these kinds of words before, but it felt different today because lawmakers were working harder than ever to change the terms of freedom. Nothing was for sure in this time, and they'd all heard stories of people losing everything and going to slavery because it was the only way to feed their children. She looked around.

"He's right," she added, standing and walking over to stand next to her uncle. "Our land provides for us and gives us the strength and opportunity to continue. Not everyone has that. Too many others have lost hope."

Everyone is quiet now, thinking about people who left the state.

William puts his hand on her shoulder in agreement with her words. He's always admired Polly's willingness to speak up when most women would not. "We have our freedom. And we own this land," he says. "We can't ever forget the price that was paid for it. That's why we get together like this; so we can tell our stories to our children. With each generation, we are richer as they pick up where we leave off, doing their part to preserve and extend both our land and our freedom."

Everyone cheers and clap. William is pleased. He's always had a way with words, but his intentions in using them has always been the same — to make sure their heritage is secured from one generation to the next.

Polly sees that the children are getting restless with the seriousness of the conversation and reaches for her gourd fiddle. Others take the cue and reach for their instruments, and soon, everyone is enjoying themselves with shared music, laughter, and dancing.

Morgan has called a mid-afternoon meeting in the judicial office. He is sitting in his private office and has a few minutes yet. He is enjoying a glass of bourbon before the legislative session. He stares deep into the amber liquid, contemplating how much he's accomplished since his early days with the legislature. Then, he was the errand runner, not anymore. He'd inherited his father's plantation nearly 20 years ago and used the status and size of his plantation to establish himself as one of Charleston's most powerful men. Now, instead of being the young man sitting on the chair next to Abram the previous chairman, he leads the legislative group.

Morgan considers himself as an authority. He's convinced he knows everything there is to know about the problems caused by free blacks and slaves who freely travel around Charleston. He knows that the only city with more free blacks in the south is New Orleans.

He knows that the population of free blacks has increased greatly since the first census. Then, the number of free blacks had been relatively small. But he saw on the 1800 and 1810 censuses the number of free blacks had greatly increased since the American Revolution, many slaves who fought against the British were emancipated for their services. Now, a larger percent of the city's population are free blacks. Most moved to the city because it was easier to find work or start a business as a tailor, barber, butcher, cook or seamstress in the cities, trades they'd learned while being slaves. Than it was to eke out a living peddling wood, vegetables or liquors in rural areas.

Morgan knew the importance of the laws that protected slavery. Another part of the problem was that many of the free blacks purchased property.

Free negroes, mulattoes, and mestizos, are entitled to all the rights of property, and protection in their persons and property, by action or indictment, which the white inhabitants of this state are entitled to.

They may purchase, hold, and transmit, by descent, real estate. ---They can mortgage, aliene, or devise the same. They may sue, and be sued...

Source: The Negro law of South Carolina, collected and digested. Suggested laws by John Belton O' Neall, 1848, Section 45 and 47.

When the young man finally knocks on Morgan's door to let him know everyone has arrived, Morgan walks into the room and takes his place at the head of table, sitting with his back to the city of Charleston. In the quiet, he declares, "Gentlemen, as you know, we still have a pressing issue to deal with. We are hearing more and more from citizens who fear for their safety. Maybe they're right to be afraid. We've heard of small uprising by slaves taking place in our neighboring counties, and we don't have a method of protecting our families should there be a large one.

"Right now, the slaves are unaware that they outnumber the white population. Although they fear our guns, we can't count on that for salvation. If the free blacks come to the knowledge of how outnumbered we are, what's to stop them from passing this information onto slaves while filling their heads with thoughts of joining forces and revolting against us?"

The solemn faced men gesture in understanding. It wasn't as if anyone in this room was going to publicly announce the dangerous tipping point the city and state were approaching, but they couldn't guarantee that the knowledge would remain a secret either.

"Well Gentlemen," Morgan continued, "I think it's fair to say that we have to figure out a way to address this."

Johnson responds in a low voice. "My wife is very nervous with all of them around. She used to feel safe while in town, but now she wants me or somebody to escort her. What if we brought in more white slaves?"

Morgan rests his cigar on the edge of a crystal ashtray and pointedly stares at Johnson. "Don't use that term again. They are not "white" slaves. They are indentured servants who will be free at the end of their term," Morgan says before leaning back in his chair, sure that he's made his point.

Johnson tries to recover. "What I mean to say, is what if we brought in more *indentured* servants from England?"

"It's not a permanent solution but increasing the number of whites in Charleston might provide some relief," Morgan says attentively.

"Perhaps," Phillip adds a thought, "but who's to say which side they'd be on if there was an uprising? It could be that bringing in more indentured servants will increase the number of people ready to take action against us. They might see it as an opportunity to get out of the terms of their agreement."

Johnson responds. "If an indentured servant tried to end their agreement, they risk becoming a slave and if they have a child, it would be born a slave.

Phillip reminds them. "The original intent of the law that a child born carries the status of the mother, was to perpetually keep blacks in slavery because their mothers would always be slaves no other country has this form of slavery."

Chapter 1, the status of the Negro, his rights and disabilities... the offspring to follow the condition of the mother...

Chapter II. The issue of a white woman and a negro, is a mulatto within the meaning of the term, and is subject to all the disabilities of the degraded caste, into which his color thrust him. The rule "partus sequitur ventrem" makes him a free man.

The result of mingling the white and negro blood is to make him a mulatto, and that carries with it, the disqualification heretofore pointed out.

The Negro law of South Carolina, collected and digested. Suggested interpretations of laws by John Belton O' Neall, 1848.

The men look to Morgan. "Nonetheless, we need to increase the number of whites in our district, even if it's just as an eye pleaser. Doing so would considerably ease the minds of our citizens. We don't want our white citizens moving to another state because they're afraid."

Johnson has a baffled look on his face. "Every year, the number of whites willing to accept the terms of an indentured agreement decreases. Instead, they go to the north with fewer slave uprisings to worry about."

Morgan replies decisively. "There are plenty of whites in Liverpool, England, and Germany living in extreme poverty. If we entice them with the idea of attaining both land and wealth in return for their servitude, they could be urged."

In the quiet produced by Morgan's statement, Philip adds, "To make sure this works out the way we foresee, there must be a law that forbids free blacks and Indians from owning white indentured servants, some of them owned white slaves in Virginia. Because our white citizens are surely distressed whenever they hear of such a thing happening, a law like this would help ease their minds."

In 1670 Virginia Assembly forbade free African Americans and Indians from owning white servants.

Source: [Hening, Statutes at Large, II:280]

It's a tranquil morning, at the breaking of dawn, Johnson's brother, Joseph, is preparing for a trip to the Ellison Plantation. Joseph is a short man with lots of facial hair and a sour expression that matches his brother's. He's made this trip for several years, and he hates it every time.

He does the best he can for his wife and family, but he and his wife argue often because he struggles to provide for the family year-round. During planting and harvest he makes sufficient money, but the months in between are sparse. They have little money to make it through long winter months.

He's angry because he is about to make another trip that will put him in debt before he's even planted a seed. Agitated that his seeds will come from a black man, as will the slave labor he'll need to hire. There are other slave owners he could turn to — white ones — but the truth is that he can't afford to go to them.

Joseph is not alone in those conditions. He and a couple of his neighbors are standing together, gazing out over the acres of untilled land stretching out before them as the first few shafts of sunlight break the horizon. They are all hoping for a prosperous year. Together, they work to hitch a rambunctious mule to the wagon; it's kicking and fighting like a dog being put in a bucket of cold water. The men steady the mule while Joseph slowly pushes the wagon forward until the latch drops into place.

A couple hours later, the men pass by the fields of Pendarvis plantation. A large number of slaves are already working, preparing the soil for planting. It's early in spring, today, the sun is hot and unforgiving as it climbs higher into the sky. When they reach the end of the long dusty dirt road, they stop to look around. Not far away stands the plantation's main house. It's not a big house by plantation standards. It's only one floor, and even at a distance Joseph can see the white paint fading to grey and peeling away.

The front door of the house swings opens, and a large man walks toward them. Pendarvis is a tall domineering colored man well respected - even by the upper-class whites in his community. The only other blacks he associates with are the Turks, many people don't consider the Turks to be blacks, even they proclaim themselves to be Portuguese.

"Joseph how are you this year?" the big man asks extending a calloused hand. "Last year you had a good harvest with your corn and potatoes. Is that your plan for this year?"

"It may even be better than last year's considering how cold this winter was. That usually means plenty of rain in the summer, so this year I'm planting beans, cabbage, and corn."

"Grab what you need. As you know, the bill for seeds or any equipment and supplies you use won't be due until the end of harvest. Everything you'll need is in the barn."

Joseph hesitates to ask his next question. "We also need to hire out five slaves. Do you have any we can use for a few months?"

"I'm sure we can work that out. Talk to my wife when you're finished loading and she will settle a contract with you."

Joseph rubs his beard. "Much oblige," he says as he and the other men walk the wagon towards the barn.

A few days later, dark clouds trail across the sky, filled with rain, and people are hastening along the streets hoping to reach their destinations before it pours.

William wants the horses pulling the buggy to go faster, but the cobblestone street is too uneven. Nicole, his great niece, is holding an umbrella over her head. He and his brother Daniel are settling for their hats protecting them. They reach Charleston's courthouse before the rain.

Walking through the front doors, Nicole observes the hustle and stir of the people doing business. She sees a couple dressed for a wedding, and farmers standing at counters filling out paperwork. She also sees the door where free blacks pay their taxes.

Daniel sees Nicole smooth out her skirt and pat her hair to make sure it's all in place. "You look kind of dressed up today. Is there a reason?" Daniel asks with a grin. He's teasing her, and she knows it.

"No particular reason," she says.

They walk along the spacious hallway, stopping at the door with a sign that says, "Wills and Documents." As they enter, the clerk looks up from her work. It's Henrietta, Johnson's wife. She looks back down at the paperwork in front of her rather than look at them.

"Well?" she asks.

Daniel starts. "I'm here to write a will."

Henrietta shuts the file in front of her. Without saying anything, she heads back to the attorney's office. When she comes back, she goes to a filing cabinet, pulls out a piece of paper, and puts it down on her desk in front of Daniel.

"Take this and sit over there," she says pointing to a bench.

Daniel picks up the paper, and the three take a seat. Before long, Richard Bourge, a French Huguenot lawyer, enters the room. Richard has spent most of his life in Charleston, he and his family had immigrated to South Carolina to escape the religious persecution taking place in their home country when he was eight years old.

Richard recognizes them and motions them to the long rectangular table in the middle of the room. He has helped the Eady family with documents on many occasions. He is pleased to see Nicole has joined them.

"What a pleasant surprise to see you again Nicole. Let's all sit," he says, holding out a chair for Nicole.

Once seated, Daniel gives the paperwork to Richard. "I'm here to complete my last will and testament."

"Have you considered what you want it to say?" Richard asks.

"I wrote down some things."

While Daniel is searching his pockets for the paper, Richard takes a glance at Nicole, easily returning the smile he finds on her face.

Daniel hands the paper over to Richard who reads it over. They talk over the details, and then Richard calls Henrietta over. "These are the details of the will," he says, handing the papers to her. "Daniel, you can come back on Wednesday of next week to sign it."

I call myself a "free coloured man" on this 10 September 1834, St. John's Parish, Charleston, Berkeley County will, proved 21 December 1834. I leave my plantation and four slaves to my daughter Esther Bluit, two slaves to my granddaughter Elizabeth Peigler, I name my nephew Jonathan Eady my executor.

Source: Free African Americans in NC VA and SC, Paul Heinegg.

They all stand and walk towards the door, both Richard and Nicole staying behind. "It's been about two months since we've met now," Richard says.

Nicole raises her head to look up at him.

"Perhaps I'll see you again?" Richard asks, his tone hopeful.

Nicole eyes meet his, "Perhaps."

shadow of Liberty

In a small downtown shoemaker's shop, George is stitching leather on a shoe. His customers were always telling him he was the best shoemaker in Charleston. He didn't know if that was true, but he did his best every time. He'd learned his craft as an apprentice, starting when he was around sixteen years old, and right from the start, the owner had been impressed with his work. Years later when the shop-owner's sight had begun to fail, he'd offered George to run the shop in return for a share of the profits.

Satisfied with the shoe, he placed it next to the others on the shelves behind his workbench and sighed. There was more empty space than there were shoes and it had been that way for a while. Being one of Charleston's better shoemakers had led to many profitable years, lately, there'd been a drop in business—and customers.

The door to his shop opens, and one of his regular customers enters. "Jacob. Good to see you."

Jacob walks to the counter stacked with leather and pulls a pair of shoes out of a bag and puts them on the counter. "I've got these shoes. I think there's still some years left in them, the soles are giving me trouble staying on."

George keenly looks at the shoes. The front door opens, and a thin serious-looking white man wearing a tight-fitting blue suit walks in. Both George and Jacob look in his direction and then back at the shoes.

"Not to worry Jacob. I can fix these. If you're in town for a while, I can have them ready for you later today."

"That'll be fine George." Jacob says turning and walking out the door.

Any other time, George would have enjoyed small talk with Jacob. He was one of a core group of loyal customers who'd been bringing their shoes—and sometimes other leather goods—to this shop for years. Some, like Jacob, had started coming in with their parents when they were children. A few had been coming to this shop before George had even begun his apprenticeship. They were all good people, and their continued patronage helped his business survive the lean months.

"Good day Sir. How can I help you?" George asks.

"I'm the new tax collector as of five months ago," Johnson states in an icy tone as he casts an unforgiving eye around the shop. "The tax records show that your business has been late and even missed payments."

"Well… there's been a drop in business over the past few months," George says, letting the implication hang in the air, not sure if the new tax collector somehow knows the reason. "I run my business the best I can, not causing any trouble…. And I always get my taxes paid."

"I met a man that looked mixed-blooded like you years ago. His last name was Edey. Is he any kin to you?"

"Might be," George said with a suspicious expression. He knew the man was talking about Daniel. "What's his first name?"

"Daniel."

George leans against the counter. "He's my cousin."

"I figured you'd be related," Johnson says rubbing his mustache. "And how about you, do you own any land?"

George is reluctant to the question and answers hesitantly. "My property is near the Santee Canal."

Johnson taps his pen on the tax book, his eyes narrowing. He then looks on the property tax list. "I see your property taxes are late too."

George sits down knowing that it's true. "The old tax collector would let me run a few months behind every now and then. He knew I always paid my taxes when they were due when business was steady."

"Well, I'm the collector now," Johnson says in a chilling tone, turning and heading towards the door, then stopping to stare at George. "Free black seamen who come to port are being put in jail for violation of entering the state and they act like they own the place. This sends the wrong message to the slaves who are there, just like you sending the wrong message with a business.". "It's not a good thing to be late with your taxes while I'm around, so get accustomed to paying your taxes when they are due or you won't have a shop."

The morning sun gleams through the branches of an oak tree, two huge boiling pots the height of a yard-fence is readied for washing clothes. It's Saturday morning, and every Saturday morning the women gather to wash clothes. Today, Daniel's wife Jemima, Polly, and Amy are sharing the chores.

There's a gentle breeze blowing that will help the clothes dry quicker, so the women are working at a steady pace to get the clothes washed, wrung out, and hung to dry. They talk while they work, happy to have something new to talk about.

The women stop and then wave at a buggy headed their way. It's one of their neighbors, Emily, who regularly brings her wash over on Saturday mornings.

"I know I'm late," she says, hefting the first of two sacks filled with clothes out of the buggy. "It was hard work trying to get pass the young'un, she stood crying at the door."

"Her cousins, are visiting today, they helped to lure her back inside."

Amy opens her mouth to say something; it's Polly who speaks up first. "You know Nicole's been seeing a lot of a lawyer lately?"

"What lawyer?" Emily asks.

"He's the lawyer who wrote the will for Daniel. She met him at the court house, he seems to like her," Polly answers while pulling the last shirt out of the water so Emily can start adding hers.

"When did Daniel write a will?" Emily asked.

"About three months ago," Polly responds. Polly and Jemima look at each other and deepen their voices imitating Daniel. "I'm a free colored man, and I need a will," they say and then burst out in laughter.

Emily laughs too, and then notices that Nicole looks eager to say something.

"Well then... What's the news?" Emily asks looking directly at Nicole. "Your face is glowing like a midnight star."

"Last night Richard asked me to go to the New Year's ball in Charleston!"

New Year's Eve, the Charleston ballroom is filled with people who turned out in their finest formal attire. Socialites mingle while standing along the walls or while sitting at the circular tables that's been lavishly spread with an impressive collection of breads, delicatessens, and bakery. Camilla Jones a free black woman, the owner of a southern cuisine catering company prepared the food. An orchestra is filling the air with music while couples waltz around the dance floor. Both wine and liquor are freely flowing, and everybody seems to be enjoying the festivities.

Richard and Nicole are sitting at a table with one of Richard's colleagues and his wife, the men occasionally talking politics while the women talk about the fashions and the food.

Richard attempts to coax Nicole onto the dance floor. "Darling, we can't go through the entire night without at least one dance. We've been talking about dancing together for the last two months. And you've put in all that time practicing."

Nicole knew he was right, but as soon as they'd walked into the ballroom, the dream of dancing with him had quickly slipped away.

Everything was so much grander than she could have ever imagined, and there were so many people! While they were making their way to their table, a gentlemen stood to shake Richard's hand. Richard was confidently and proudly introducing her all night, and she received many friendly and polite responses in return, there was no denying that there were people who didn't approve of her being there. She saw it on some of their faces, and as she discretely looked around the room hoping to find another person of color, she realized that every guest was white—at least outwardly.

Richard put a finger under Nicole's chin, gently raising her head until he could look into her eyes. She looks back into his feeling her resolve weakening, remembering how wonderful she imagined it would be dancing with him at the New Year's Ball. Richard stood and extended his hand to her. She accepted it, and he lead her to the dance floor.

Midnight is approaching; Richard and Nicole had been dancing more than a couple of hours. The band's music was more spirited and the ease of their synchronized moves began to settle Nicole's nerves. She focused only on him, letting herself forget everybody and everything else.

When the song ended Richard whispered into her ear, "You are so lovely darling!"

She felt the warmth that was always between them, and as if he could read her mind, Richard escorted her to one of the outside balconies. Midnight is getting close; Richard takes her hands in his. Both sensing how strongly they feel for each other. Both knowing as the old year was leaving; the New Year would bring them closer. Their relationship had grown regardless of their color, religion or anything else. Taking her to the Ball didn't have anything to do with social conventions. He's fallen in love with her. She danced with him because she loves and trust him even though she's the only person of color in a ball gown. He leans in and gives her a hug to bond their feelings.

A beautifully handcrafted carriage approaches the cast iron gates that stand at the entrance of Morgan's plantation on a moonless night. The carriage's driver is German; he raises an eyebrow as they pass through. He recognizes the design and knows black artisans did the work. He knows the reputation of the man in his carriage, and wonders at the fact that someone so devoted to the mission of controlling every black person in the city of Charleston would be willing to pay any of them for their skills.

As the carriage nears the house, the driver catches sight of light flickering through the slats of the smaller of two barns. If it were his barn, he'd be checking to see why there was light in the barn. He looks over his shoulder at Morgan wondering if he should say something, remembering how drunk Morgan had been when he'd picked him up outside of Charleston's tavern. He was sleeping, but he was going to have to wake up soon enough, so the driver pulled the horses to a stop. Morgan stirred, looking around as if he was trying to figure out where he was.

"Sir, there's a light inside your barn," the driver says pointing in the direction of the light. "It's late, so I thought you might like to know."

Morgan's turns his head to follow the driver's extended arm and sees the light for himself. "It's probably that damn slave girl trying to read," a drunken Morgan snarls as he hauls himself out of the carriage. The driver watches him stagger towards the barn, as he mutters.

"Damn Sunday school teachers putting ideas in their heads," Morgan says as he pushes the two barn doors open with such force that one of them hits the barn and bounces back, hitting him on his shoulder. He roars in anger and starts walking toward the light yelling. "I know you're in here. And I know what you're doing, reading one of those damn books."

Anna doesn't move because of fear. There's no place to run, no place to hide. She'd snuck out of her quarters and come here to look at the book Bristow had given her. He'd helped her sound out the words and she just had to try reading it one more time on her own before she went to sleep. She pushes the book behind her back trying to hide it from the angry voice headed her way. As the man's face comes into view, she sucks in a breath, it's not the overseer.

Morgan sees the girl sitting next to the lamp, and just as he thought, it's the girl the overseer had pointed out to him — the one who seemed determined to learn how to read and write. As he approaches, he sees the proof. A book is sticking out from behind her back. She covers herself with her thin arms as he lunges at her believing he's going to hit her.

Morgan grabs the book and waves it in the air. "This book won't do you any good," he says opening it, grabbing it with both hands, and ripping it in two. "You've been told. And you've been warned," he continues, tossing the pieces aside and looking around the barn for a way to punish her.

His eyes stop on an axe stuck in a big block of wood to his left. He frowns, grabbing the handle and freeing the axe with one quick jerk. "I bet you won't think about reading anymore books when I chop your fingers off," he yells, swinging the axe at the block, but missing it and chopping through the side of his boot on the follow through instead.

Morgan howls with both anger and pain, but Anna sees her chance to escape and takes it. He lunges at her as she runs past him, but she's too quick. At the door, she stops and looks back. *Even if you do chop them off,* she thinks, *I won't stop reading.*

Morgan tries to go after her, but stops as soon as he puts weight on his injured foot. All he can do right now is glare determinedly outside the barn. He's not done with her.

Chapter 7

Flawing in Love

A slave stops at a well to get a drink of water on the Morgan Plantation. He's tired, having spent all day toiling in the field. The water is refreshing, it's still hot outside. His shirt is soaked with the sweat of today's work, so he pulls it off hoping the breeze might provide some relief.

He is dark and muscular and in his prime. At least that's what Beth thinks. Her husband, Morgan, had bought him a few months ago. He'd gotten a good price because his previous owner didn't like the way his daughters were looking at him. It hadn't been the first time Beth had heard Morgan discuss the purchase or sale of a slave. It hadn't been the first time her Christian beliefs had come to mind either. *This kind of thing should never happen or ever be*, she'd thought. *It is ungodly for people to own slaves.*

The story of this slave had perplexed her. There were stories about masters and female slaves, and she knew from other conversations she'd overheard that on some plantations it was common for indentured servants to sleep with black slaves. She'd never heard of a free white woman choosing to sleep with a slave. Nor did she understand how a white woman could look at a slave that way.

Then she'd seen him. She had been looking out the window, saw him walk from the field, and stops for a drink of water. Maybe it was the way he stood and looked out over the horizon while he drank. Maybe it was the fact that he stood tall and strong, or that he didn't walk with his head down.

Soon, she is waiting for him on a daily basis, always standing just off to the side of the window, battling her beliefs and her desires. She was the lady of the plantation. She was married, but in truth, her marriage was far from what she had hoped it would be. Yes, her husband was one of Charleston's most prestigious citizens, and she enjoys many comforts because of his position, she has paid a price for those comforts.

Beth was many years younger than Morgan, and though he had been charming in the beginning, those pretenses had been left behind several years ago—even more so after the birth of their son. Morgan drinks regularly, and with all the talk of an uprising, Beth has given in to having a glass of sherry or wine to steady her nerves on the evenings he is gone.

The first time she drinks more than a glass it makes her sick to her stomach and causes a horrible headache the next morning. She vows to herself that she will never do it again, there was still talk of an uprising, Morgan was still gone most of the time, and a drink—or two—did make it easier to cope. With little else to occupy her time, she lately finds herself standing off to the side of this window in the afternoon wondering if the man by the well would keep her safe if there were an uprising. Today, that question joins another familiar question. What would it be like to touch him?

In another minute she knew he would turn and walk away, and today, for some reason, it was a thought that spurs her to action. She steps in front of the open window and calls out to him. "Hey…. Bring me some water." She blushes as soon as the words were out of her mouth. It was a brash thing to do, but she was also embarrassed that it had sounded so much like a command.

Troy hears the voice, turns towards it, and see her standing at the window. He'd seen her there before and knew who she was. She was Beth, Morgan's wife. She was clearly younger than her husband. Her skin was a pale creamy white, and her hair was long and black. She moves away from the window, but within a few seconds, the front door opens.

He didn't say anything. He rinses the metal cup, fills it with the cool water and carries it to her. At the front door, he extends the cup towards her.

"Oh," she says, looking down at his hand. "It's not for me, it's for my plants. I was just noticing they need water and I saw you by the well, and… thought to ask," she said almost apologetically.

Troy nodds and went back to the well to fill a bucket with water, remembering something Anna, one of the young slave girls, had told him about Mrs. Morgan. She said she'd seen her watching him. He'd laughed, Anna had shaken her head and said Mrs. Morgan had been watching him for a while now, and she was sure Mrs. Morgan was thinking about him "that way."

After Anna had told him, he'd taken notice of Beth. Not when he was at the well, other times when she was in her buggy, riding by the field on her way into the city. Or when she was sitting in the garden keeping an eye on her son while he was playing. That was it. Surely, Anna had been mistaken, and even if she wasn't, nothing good could ever come out of paying the master's wife any mind or attention.

When Troy returns to the front porch, Beth led him through to the sitting room, pointing out the plants that needs watering. He went about the task carefully so as not to spill the water, noticing a nearly empty glass of wine on a side table. Seeing it made him angry. It's wrong that she should be alone so much that a drink becomes comfort.

They walk through the rooms with Troy stopping to water the plants along the way. He has plenty of water because the plants aren't really dry and don't really need watering. The last room they go into is a small bedroom. Troy is nervous because the room is so small. He goes to pour the water into one of the plants and overfills it, spilling water onto the sill. Beth is quick with a handkerchief, accidentally brushing against him as she reaches towards the spill.

The two stop, and for the first time look at each other. Beth can feel her heart starting to race, a response to his strong and sure presence. She looks into his eyes he is returning her gaze, her hand coming to rest on the back of his. His eyes are a warm deep brown.

Troy feels the touch, he doesn't flinch. "Ma'am, let me get something to wipe the sill," he says, but doesn't move. Instead, he falls into the haze of her hazel eyes, his body responding to the touch of her hand.

Neither one of them moves for a while, each one taking in the look of the other. Beth reaches up and gently brushes aside a bead of sweat trickling down Troy's forehead. He takes her hand in his, their fingers entwining with ease.

Beth can feel her desire growing. She's never felt like this before. She doesn't want to let it go, and slides her arms around his neck. In turn, Troy wraps his strong arms around her. Their lips brush against one another's lightly as if each were testing the level of the other's desire. There was no question to answerer. No difference to keep them apart, just desire and consent.

On a restful Sunday afternoon, Bristow Jr. walks down a dirt road that skirts the backside of the Morgan plantation, the side with the slaves. He sees Anna sitting on a tree stump out by the barn and walks over to her with a smile on his face. "How was church today?"

Anna shrugs. She'd just gotten back a short while ago. She's drawing circles and straight lines in the dirt with a crooked stick. "The preacher was talkin' about the promise land," she says without interest. She is occupied with her own thoughts during services, *"I know God ain't unjust and he didn't make dem white folks no better than me."* Then she asks, "Bristow is dem white folks going to be in heaven, since they don't want us to read? Oh, never mind." "Bristow?" She starts again, looking up at him with a hopeful expression. She has heard her mother and others say they can't read or write but they want their children to. "What's it like to write?"

Bristow Jr. beams. He is sometimes hot-tempered but not around her. He likes to talk to Anna. She's always asking him questions he can answer. He likes this question a lot because he's proud of the fact that he can read and write, and he's only 12 years old. Not everyone can, as strange as it seems to him. "It feels good I guess…. But I can show you how to write and then you'll know for yourself," he says, walking around until he finds a stick for himself. "Why do you want to write?"

"I wanna write a story. I wanna see what I say on paper, and feel proud that I put the words on the paper myself—like the stories I hear in the bible." She shrugs again. "I just have all these words in me and don't know how they look. And you know what?" she asks. Bristow shakes his head. "I wanna write myself free! I don't wanna be a slave. I want my promised land."

Bristow Jr. understands. Writing is a kind of freedom. There are plenty of people who don't want blacks to be able to read and write—especially when it comes to their slaves. They think being able to read and write will give their slaves ideas, but even those who can't read and write have ideas. Nothing can stop ideas. But if you can read and write, it sure is a lot easier to share them.

"Ok," Bristow Jr. says. "Watch what I do with my stick and you do the same thing."

Bristow Jr. writes Anna's name in the dirt while she carefully follows his lead. When she's done, she looks at him. "What's it say?"

"It says Anna," he tells her. "See? A – N – N – A. Anna."

Anna squeals with excitement. "Show me some more!"

They practice for a while, Anna humming as she follows Bristow Jr.'s lead. Then she catches sight of the overseer heading in their direction and quickly brushes her bare feet over the letters before he can see them.

The overseer stares at the two as he approaches. Anna doesn't say anything. She just gets up and runs to change her clothes before she heads to the main house to help with dinner.

Bristow Jr. heads back to the road and walks home.

Just past one o'clock, Nicole arrives at the Pineville Race Track with her uncle Bristow. She can't see the track, but she can hear people cheering louder and louder, and the sound of horse's hoofs hitting the ground.

Nicole has never been to the track on a race day. Today was different it was filled with excitement. Nicole can see the back of the spectator stands. She can also see people placing bets, while horses walked.

Nicole steps down from the buggy and takes a few steps closer to where the horses for the race are walking.

The men walking the horses are black, and she wonders how many of them are free blacks. Some of them could be, but she knows that most of them are probably slaves—even if they are jockeys. That was often the case since colonial times, horse owners and breeders figured out that horses responded better to the people who took care of them.

For weeks, people had been talking about a black jockey who was going to be in one of the races. His name was Simon, and he was one of the first former slaves to become a famous jockey. She didn't know when his race was going to take place, but she was hoping it would be while she was there.

Nicole hears someone call her name, and the cheerful thought that it sounds like Richard enters her mind. She had secretly been hoping to see him here, and when she turns around, she sees him walking towards her.

"Nicole, I thought that was you. How wonderful to see you here," looking around to see who she's with.

"I'm here with my uncle."

While they're talking, Bristow returns to the buggy and looks around for Nicole. When he sees her standing by the track talking to someone, he gets close enough to see that she's talking to Richard, who he knows to be a respectable gentleman.

Bristow see's the two of them looking fondly at each other. He waves his hand and shouts, "Nicole, see you after the race."

Nicole lifts her voice and says, "Okay, Uncle Bristow see you soon."

Then he decides it's proper to walk over and converses with Mr. Richard Bourge and to let Nicole know where to meet him after the race.

After the conversation Richard says, "Let me show you what the track is all about."

Nicole listens to Richard as he begins to tell her what he knows about the horses. She knows a bit about horse racing because she'd seen a few races when she was much younger. But, nothing on this scale.

"Have you ever seen a horse race up close?"

"Never like this," admits Nicole. "Is it always this exciting?"

"It can be. There are many good horses here today, so there's a lot at stake for some of the people here. It's very different by the track than it is here."

"Really?" "Oh yes, so close I could jump on a horse," he says, teasing her just a little. "I do have close seats, so you'll get to see firsthand."

Seated closely, the two watch the next race, and then fill the long stretch of time until the next race with easy conversation about their families, hopes for the future, laughter, and the occasional touch on the hand or arm.

The rail swiftly lifts, when the horses are in position for the next race. The race begins, with horses running forward and hooves pounding along the track.

The announcer's voice keeps reaching new heights as he yells from atop a tall makeshift stage. "*Take You Home* has a steady lead!"

"Forget about Simon," Richard says in a playful voice. "I'm going for that one!"

The announcer yells again, "*Not Tonight* is moving up to challenge *Take You Home* and they are neck and neck!"

"I'm rooting for that one!" Nicole laughs.

The horse Simon is riding is three lengths back at the halfway point, but with each powerful stride, he is gaining ground. All the jockeys are pushing their horses with all their might towards the finish line. Simon is third, but quickly moves up the inside into second.

Richard and Nicole are both on their feet shouting, watching Simon steadily urging his thoroughbred. At the three-quarter mark, Simon is challenging for the lead while the crowd cheers louder than ever. When the horses cross the finish marker, Simon finishes second to *Take You Home.*

Overtaken in the excitement of the moment, Richard wraps his arms around Nicole, lifts her up, and kisses her on the lips!

Chapter 8

Property Deeds

A man dressed in a dark suit with a white shirt and skinny black tie stands outside a brick building in Charleston. He lifts a lantern above his head as a group of men walk towards him. The light from the lantern illuminates a sign. It reads, "Brown's Fellowship Society." It was founded thirty years earlier in the late 1700's to educate members and their children, to provide insurance and burial grounds. Some of the founding members were a group of free blacks from Saint-Domingue, who fled the French colony during the successful Toussaint Louveture rebellion against slavery. Those who wanted to flee the turmoil boarded ships leaving for America and landed at ports in Savannah and Charleston.

He greets them with handshakes, pats on the back and ushers them through the door, directing them to a concrete staircase at the back of the entryway.

In a downstairs room, members have gathered for their monthly meeting, after hearing disturbing rumors they tensely mingle. As the hour approaches, they begin to fill the chairs organized into rows. The small windows have curtains drawn over them and are barely visible from the street.

All the men have light-skin complexions, they maintain their calm. They've heard about a possible law which would cause free blacks to return to slavery or leave the state. They are uncertain of their families' futures.

The president of the society, Elias, enters the room pausing to hang up his black trench coat. His confidence and manners are evident in the way he casually walks to the front of the room and takes his place behind the podium. The members begin to settle, their voices fading into silence.

"Since the founding of our organization," Elias begins, "We have never been involved in any of the political issues of this city and have managed our issues well. However, city legislators are proposing a law for free blacks to return to slavery or leave the state."

A presentment from the grand jury who wanted free blacks to leave the state or return to slavery.

Presentment of Grand Jury extra term,

The jury present the accumulation of free Negros amongst us as a serious and in many ways an alarming evil, begetting in our midst an idle and profligate people whose worst influences tend to the corrupting of the slave population. The integrity of our institution requires… that all free Negros be compelled to leave the state: or in default of this, to choose their masters and then return to a manner of life better suited to their own nature, more conducive to their permanent well being, and contributing more effectually to the common prosperity and the public safety.

Source: South Carolina Department of Archives and History.

Elias pauses briefly to look around the silent room. "If this law passes, it will shatter our lives. We are a people straddling between freedom and bondage. We must exist between these two worlds, but as in other times. We will find a way to prevail against this cruel law. We can – and we will – take this matter to court."

A hush holds the room caged like an exotic bird. The silence fades as individuals begin to whisper louder as questions begin to form.

An elderly man, with uncertainty lingering in his voice, "What has provoked them to write this malicious petition?"

Others tensely sit and voice their desire to hear an answer. Elias raises one hand to settle the crowd before answering. "Look around the city on your travels and you will see the answer. Each census shows an increase in our numbers. The whites believe we are a danger to the institution of slavery and want a way to get rid of us. I just received a newspaper from Jehu Jones while he was visiting New York. This same upheaval is happening in other states."

The telegram informs us that Gov. Stewart, of Missouri, has vetoed the bill passed by the legislature expelling free negroes from the State under penalty of being reduced to slavery…Yet several of the Southern States are still busy with schemes for reducing all the free negroes within their limits, with their offspring, to perpetual slavery….In nearly all of the Southern States, steps are in progress for expelling them or for reducing them to servitude….Many of them have lived blameless lives, have raised and educated families, and have accumulated property,--contributing their share to sustain the burdens of Society, and obeying all its laws…The dangers of having a class of free negroes in a Slave State are sometimes urged as an excuse for such legislation....

Source: New York Times.

> Presentment of the Grand Jury…
>
> They would also recommend that some action in regard to the free negroes in our State be taken by Legislature as their presence among us is regarded as injurious to the slaves.
>
> REUBEN BURRESS, Foreman

Source: South Carolina Department of Archives and History.

Richard DeReef a founder of the society asks. "Do you think this petition will become a law?"

Elias replies quickly and firmly. "I have been told a bill has been written, they have given it much consideration. However, the same courthouse where this bill was written will be the same court house we present our case."

The members begin to respond with pledges of support to Elias, and to each other. A man stands and waits until Elias looks at him before he timidly asks, "If we get involved with this by going to court, will we be in danger of slavery? We do live in a peculiar city."

"We have a right to take a stand, however there maybe acts of retaliation by other laws being written." Elias tells them.

"If this bill is signed, it will be another law meant to make us believe that there is no place for free blacks. Leaving is not an answer. If we leave, there will be laws in other states waiting for us, this is our home as much as it is theirs."

The members stand, ready to commit to what has to be done. Elias takes control and calms the crowd. When they are quiet, he continues. "As much as we have tried

to create peace and not cause problems, we now face this uncertainty. We formed this society to educate, protect, help the enslaved and have a burial ground. We will continue to do these things. I have written a petition about our concerns and it is here for you to sign, and we have help from some good white citizens."

A petition written by white citizens who wanted free blacks to continue living in the state, it tells of free blacks owning property worth more than half a million dollars. A copy of the original petition follows.

> *The petition of the undersigned citizens of Charleston respectfully sheweth(show). That they have seen with regret in the papers the draught of a bill professing to drive out free coloured people from the state...*
>
> *Your petitioners can find no reason for such severity on the contrary they believe the project one of wrong and injustice to a class of inhabitants who ought to be objects of our care and protection.*
>
> *We perceive prose many among them who command the respect of all respectable men, many who are good citizens...*
>
> *There can be no better proof of this than the fact that they hold property in the city of Charleston to the value of more than half a million of dollars.*
>
> *Their laborer ...to us in this neighborhood. They are the only workmen who will or can take employment in the county during the summer. We cannot build or repair a house in that season without the use of the coloured carpenter or bricklayer...*

Source: South Carolina Department of Archives and History.

Source: South Carolina Department of Archives and History.

To the Honble
The President and Members
of the Senate of South Carolina

The petition of the undersigned citizens of Charleston respectfully showeth, That they have seen with regret in the papers, the draught of a bill proposing to drive our free coloured people from the State under the heaviest penalties.

Your petitioners can find no reason for such severity. on the contrary, they believe the project one of wrong and injustice to a class of our inhabitants who ought to be objects of our care and protection.

We know many among them who command the respect of all respectable men, many who are good citizens, patterns of industry, sobriety, and irreproachable conduct. There can be no better proof of this than the fact that they hold property in the City of Charleston to the value of more than half a million of Dollars.

Their labour is indispensable to us in this neighbourhood. They are the only work men who will, or can, take employment in the Country during the summer. We cannot build or repair a house in that season without the use of the coloured carpenter or bricklayer.

But we put their claim to protection on a higher ground. In their humble station they are equitably entitled to the rights which the laws of their native place have secured to them. These may be properly called vested
rights

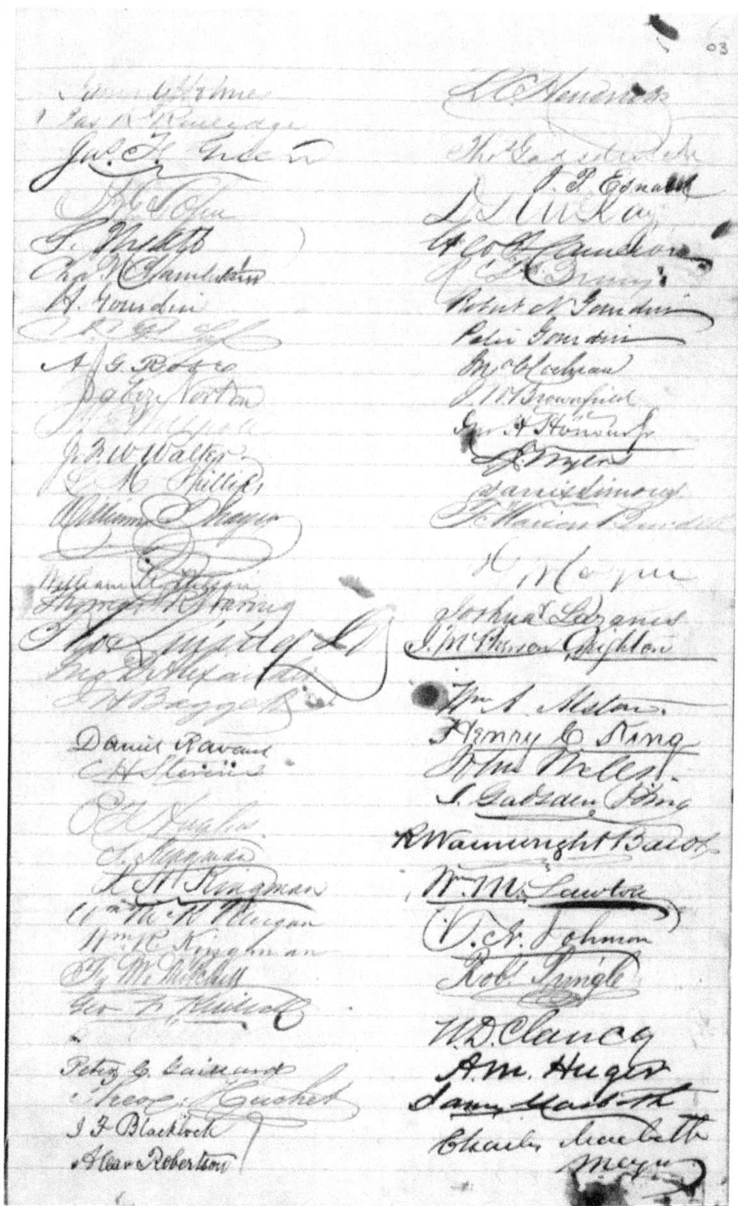

Source: South Carolina Department of Archives and History.

Free blacks petitioned against laws and took matters
to court. For example, free blacks came and went from the
state before laws prevented them from returning to the

state if they left. Such was the case for Jehu Jones, a prominent free black real estate owner in Charleston. He used the large profits he'd made from tailoring to invest in the hotel industry. He left the state to visit his wife and family in New York. Several "free persons of color" and a white citizen had to petition the court before Jones could return.

A petition to allow Jehu Jones to return to the state of South Carolina, it has signatures of free persons of color on a copy of the original petition that follows.

To the Honorable Senate and House of Representative of the State of So.Carolina.

The undersigned respectfully represent to your honorable body that they are citizens of Charleston that they have seen the petition of Jehu Jones praying to be permitted to return to So. Carolina. That from their knowledge of the said Jehu Jones while a resident of this city formally and from the certificate of Col. Drayton as well as from information received from various persons who have recently seen and conversed with him they are fully satisfied that his character is fair and his departments such as to render him not merely harmful but exceedingly well calculated to diffuse useful knowledge and inculcate proper principles in our coloured population- The undersigned therefore cordially join in recommending that the prayer of his petition be granted-

Source: South Carolina Department of Archives and History.

To the Hon Senate and House of Representatives of the State of South Carolina

The undersigned respectfully represent to your Honorable Body that they are Citizens of Charleston — That they have seen the petition of Jehu Jones praying to be permitted to return to South Carolina. That from their knowledge of the said Jehu Jones while a resident of this city formerly, & from the certificate of Col Drayton as well as from information received from various persons who have recently seen & conversed with him, they are fully satisfied that his character is fair, & his deportment such as to render him not merely harmless, but exceedingly well calculated to diffuse useful knowledge & inculcate proper principles in our colored population. They The undersigned, therefore, cordially join in recommending that the prayer of his petition be granted.

Joseph Manigault.
Jacob Bond I'On
James Rose
James Gadsden.
Alfred Huger
Edward M. Crady
H. Gourdin
John Y. Stock
Richard Yeadon Junr.
W. Hampton
James Legare
William Bull

Thos. Ashby
F. Tupper
Ja. McMullen
J. E. Brandon
Charles Reynolds
J. Edward Calhoun
John B. Irving
Wm. Lucas
F. W. Baird
Alexander Mazyck
Vardry McBee
J. Seyer Hutchinson

Source: South Carolina Department of Archives and History.

A petition by free people of color, members of a Methodist church in Charleston wanting to purchase property.

> *To the honorable, the Speaker and Members of the House of Representatives of the State of South Carolina.*
>
> *The humble Petition of the subscribers respectfully sheweth (show)*
>
> *That your Petitioners who are free persons of color, on behalf of themselves and others of the religious sect or denomination called Methodist in the City of Charleston, are desirous of purchasing two lots of land to appropriate us a place of internment for themselves and their descendants: the present burial ground being inadequate for that purpose…*

Source: South Carolina Department of Archives and History.

Joseph and Richard Edward DeReef, two successful free men of color in 19th-century Charleston. The brothers obtained their wealth through the purchase of real estate and establishing a lumber factory…. The brothers were founding members of the Brown Fellowship Society…

Source: College of Charleston, Special Collections.

The slaves purchased by Joseph and Richard Edward DeReef were elderly, infants, couples, mothers and daughters and cripples according to bills of sales, this suggest they were purchased for benevolent reasons.

Source: Bill of sales, SC Department of Archives and History.

Chapter 9

Freedom Papers

Wayward trees sway in the wind near an unplowed field, the dirt road is slim and long. William and Daniel ride their wagon, they're almost home. William begins talking about his visit with George at the shoe shop.

"I was talking to George at his shop today," William said, looking over the field of weeds. "He was talking about his business being slow and he may have to close his shop. He knows there is a great demand from plantation owners who need shoes for their slaves, but he wouldn't be able to fill the orders unless he bought and slaves as apprentices. There is no one else to do the labor he can afford to pay. This is the challenge of free black shoemakers, barbers, hairdressers and bakers who refuse to buy bondsmen."

William folds his arms. "George gave his opinion about slavery, saying, "If I could end slavery it would end by nightfall.""

Daniel responds, shifting the reigns of the horse to only one hand. "That's a thought I've been pondering."

"Yesterday a runaway said he watched from the woods before he approached my land. His owner had recently sold his wife because he needed to pay a debt. He then decided to run away. He'll risk being caught if he stays too long, he knows other farmers who needs help, who don't agree with the system of slavery. He was a peddler for his master, so he knows his way around the countryside."

Daniel then says, "After I left the courthouse, I found emancipation papers were accidentally mixed in with my will, but I believe on purpose. Mr. Richard Bourge gave me the papers and I still have them in my drawer. I know someone who can fill it out, afterwards I'll give them to the runaway."

Their lives hadn't changed much, but the world around them seems to be in a constant state of unrest.

There was a lot of talk among black slave owners about freeing their slaves. "There was a time when I followed the way of the south. It was the way I knew to make a living for my family." The fact that he "owned" three people had begun to weigh on his mind.

He didn't think about them as "slaves," at least not in the way most people did. Like most colored slave owners, he owned less than eight slaves. They weren't treated like the slaves he had seen all those years ago when they'd ridden through the Pendarvis Plantation. His slaves weren't treated as what he saw on large plantations. He'd never forgotten the look of hopelessness on the faces of the men who stared in their direction as they'd passed by. He watched for it after that day, he hadn't seen that look on their faces, not once in all the years that had passed. Still, times were changing, and he began to question his ownership of slaves.

"It's like we live in two worlds," Daniel continues. "In one, we do what we have to. I couldn't compete with the price of my crops on the market, if it weren't for the work Isaac and Will do. They eat with us and talk with us, and I see them every day. But that's still in the corral of slavery and isn't the same as being free."

William agrees and briefly closes his eyes. "When I bought Ceasar, I could just as any white man, and it was my legal right to buy him.

William Edy a free black man purchased a slave named Ceasar in 1806, Charleston District. A copy of the original document follows.

State of South Carolina

KNOW ALL MEN BY THESE PRESENTS, That I Moses Bradley of the City of Charleston⋯

for and in consideration of the sum of six hundred fifty dollars___________

To me in hand paid, at and before the sealing and delivery of these presents

William Edy a Free Black Man

The receipt whereof I do hereby acknowledge, to have bargain and sold, and by these presents do bargain, sell and deliver to the said William Edy, a negro slave named Ceasar above twenty years old, late the property of Joshua Eden...

TO HAVE AND TO HOLD the said Slave Ceasar

unto the said William Edy...

State of South-Carolina.

Know all Men by these Presents, That I Moses Bradley of the City of Charleston State aforesaid [illegible] for and in consideration of the sum of Six hundred fifty Dollars to me in hand paid, at and before the sealing and delivery of these presents William Edy a Free Black Man the receipt whereof I do hereby acknowledge, to have bargained and sold, and by these presents do bargain, sell and deliver to the said William Edy a negro slave named Ceasar [illegible] [illegible] unto the said William Edy.

TO HAVE AND TO HOLD the said slave Ceasar [illegible] unto the said William Edy his executors, administrators and assigns, to him and their own proper use and behoof forever. And I the said Moses Bradley my executors and administrators, the said bargained premises unto the said William Edy his executors, administrators and assigns, from and against all persons shall and will warrant and forever defend by these presents.

IN WITNESS whereof I have hereunto set my hand and seal. Dated in Charleston, this [illegible] day of [illegible] in the year of our Lord one thousand eight hundred and [illegible] and of the Independence of the United States of America the twenty-[illegible]

SIGNED, SEALED AND DELIVERED IN THE PRESENCE OF [illegible]

The bill of sale for William Edy a free black man who purchases a slave named Ceasar. Source: South Carolina Department of Archives and History.

I see our world changing, where the right to own another human being should be challenged. I don't want to be a man who forgot his own roots. We would be slaves today if our ancestors hadn't fought for our freedom. They fought for us, and maybe it's time for us to fight for others freedom."

William looks up to the sky. "My hands have been put to the plows of this unjust system for long enough, and I'm letting go."

Daniel pulls the harness bringing the wagon to a halt. "We're too old to fight in a battle. We can only do what we can."

Daniel Eady is shown owning 7 slaves with 8 people in the household in the Journal of Negro History. Column 3 list ages of slaves. Esther Bluit (Blute) was his daughter.

JOURNAL OF NEGRO HISTORY

BERKELEY St. John's			
Eady, Daniel............	7	8	100–
St. Stephen's			
Blute, Hester..........	1	5	55–100

Source: The Journal of Negro History, by Carter G. Woodson.

In 1834 Daniel Eady, a colored farmer of St. John's Berkeley Parish in Charleston District, gave his daughter Esther Bluit the use of three slaves named Catherine, Isaac, and, William. When Esther Bluit died, her cousin Jonathan Eady, who used the slaves Isaac and William as field hands, inherited the slaves., Susannah Eady, the aunt of Jonathan Eady, requested that her nephew should be given her slave Mariah and all her plantation implements and livestock.

Source: Free Black Slaveowners in South Carolina 1790-1860, by Larry Koger.

Susannah Eady, a widow, left a 20 January 1807 St. John's Parish, Charleston County, South Carolina will, proved 31, May 1805 by which she asked that she be buried at her brother Daniel Eady's place in the same parish, left 5 schillings each to her siblings Daniel, William, George and Mary, left cattle to her niece Nancy and Peggy, and left a slave, plantation tools and the remainder of her property to her nephew Jonathan Eady. [Will Book E, 1807 – 17, 509].

Source: Free African Americans VA, NC and SC from Colonial Period to 1860, Paul Heinegg.

In 1850, Jonathan Eady, a colored farmer of St. Stephen's Parish in Charleston County, owned six slaves, four of whom were between 20 and 45 years old and used as field hands. His slaves tilled 100 acres of land and grew 450 bushels of Indian corn. Once Eady extracted the amount of produce needed to sustain his family and slaves, he sold the surplus...

Source: Free Black Slaveowners in South Carolina 1790-1860, by Larry Koger.

On a country hillside, the trees rustle with the waning wind. A stream of clear water flows nearby. Although it's mid-summer, the air is cool. Richard and Nicole sit by the edge of the stream, holding hands and reminiscing about how they first met.

"I'm glad your uncle was able to give you the message to meet me here. It was by chance I saw him at the courthouse." Richard says.

"I'm glad he saw you! This is such a gorgeous afternoon and meeting you here is always wonderful," Nicole says.

"We've known each other for quite a while now," Richard says, pausing a little before continuing, thinking how much he cares for her. "I have something to ask you. Nicole, my love, I have been thinking about this a lot. It is hard for me to imagine my life without you being a part of it. Darling I want you to be my wife. Will you marry me?"

Nicole is overcome with tears; she is overtaken by the moment. Barely a second passes before she proclaims her answer. "Oh, Richard! Yes!" she leaps to her feet.

Richard stands and puts his hands around her waist, leans forward and gives Nicole a kiss. The occasion made her forget about the law that forbids them from getting married, once she remembers she pulls back, as her moment of joy vanishes.

"Richard, how can it be? What about the new law that forbids blacks and whites from getting married?"

Richard reaches for her hands and steps closer. "It's true, there is a law that was just written. There's also Morgan to contend with. He has been trying to disrupt my life ever since I was able to interrupt the bill that would have caused free blacks to leave the state or return to slavery. But remember," he says with a confident smirk, "I'm a lawyer."

There were legal interracial marriages in South Carolina before it was prohibited.

They may contract, and be contracted with. Their marriages with one another, and even with white people, are legal...

The Negro Law of South Carolina, collected and digested by John Belton O' Neall, 1848, in Section 47.

> Resolved that the same committee be instructed to inquire into the expediency of prohibiting by law the marriage of a white person with a free negro and to declare all such marriages null and void and the issue of any such marriages to be illegitimate. 1845

Source: South Carolina Department of Archives and History.

Morgan takes a draw on his cigar. Once again, he is sitting in his chair in the legislative room seeing many of the chairs are empty.

He stands at the window with his back to the room staring at the busy street. Outside, there are too many blacks walking around as far as he is concerned. None of them are his... at the very least, he's sure of that. His slaves are working. His overseer sees to that.

Still, he stares at each black person trying to decide if they are a slave or a free black. There was a time when it was easy to tell, mostly light-skinned blacks were free, but those days are gone, now more dark skin blacks are free.

He watches as a group of finely dressed blacks step out of a stagecoach and wonders where they're from. They had passed a law in 1822 forbidding free blacks' entry into the state, but that law had its limits. For one, it hadn't stopped the increase of free blacks in the state. It's hard to detect runaway slaves on our streets. They use emancipation papers given to them by free blacks to use as proof of freedom and some of our white citizens forge the papers. *There must be a way;* he reminds himself, determined to find a way.

Morgan turns from the window then takes his seat at the head of the table. His lips tighten at the sight of so many empty chairs; however, he is pleased with the men who are there. They have been with him since the beginning, and they share his beliefs and concerns about slavery.

"Johnson, I see by your last report that the number of free blacks owning businesses continues to rise. "Well now," Morgan says shifting his eyes, "let's put their taxes to good use and figure out a way to end the trend."

Phillip clears his throat and waits for Morgan to acknowledge him before he speaks. "Sir there are rumors about another revolt. The Memorialist have given me word that free blacks were heard talking about Denmark Vesey and why his conspiracy to revolt had failed, and how they could improve on his plan."

Morgan waved a dismissive hand. "That was months ago, Vesey failed because even slaves know they have it better right where they are than they would on their own."

Phillip leaned back in his seat, feeling duty-bound to remind Morgan how close the city came to a devastating revolt. He wants Morgan to remember how grave the conspiracy was. "I agree. It was a while ago, but keep in mind that thousands of slaves and free blacks plotted the most elaborate conspiracy our nation has ever seen, right here in Charleston. They planned well, conspiring to revolt at a time when most of our white population was away for the summer. Their intent of attacking our ammunition might have succeeded if we hadn't received information from the Memorialist about their plan before it happened."

They all knew well what Vesey had almost accomplished. Vesey had been a slave who bought himself out of bondage and became a well to do carpenter and preacher. Vesey found followers while preaching at an African Methodist church. He was a devout Christian and used the pulpit to plant a vision that just as Moses and the Israelites had defeated their oppressors; slaves would get to their promised land. The slaves who heard him speak shared his message.

Vesey would admonish slaves who lowered their heads to white people. He became disturbed and told them to keep their heads up. "They are men, just as we are," he would say.

"Certainly, there were more white people in Charleston now, there are also more blacks," Phillip continued. "And with so many blacks walking around free, it's almost impossible to keep our slaves from wondering about freedom.

Morgan shifts his position in his chair and closes his eyes, half-heartedly nodding in agreement, choosing not to respond. The conspiracy had failed, but not totally. He knew whites were still afraid of what could happen.

Johnson's voice starts low, growing in volume as he speaks. "What we need is a better way of knowing the slaves from the free blacks. We wrote a law after the Vesey conspiracy that requires all free blacks older than sixteen to have a legal white guardian and wear a tag."

Morgan remains quiet, listening to his committee suggest ideas. He has been preoccupied with a solution of his own, taking a long draw on his cigar before he speaks. "What we could do," adding a long pause for effect, "is write a law that would prohibit blacks from meeting in groups without the presence of a white person. If they do, they will be subject to arrest. We could also restrict their ability to be on the streets during late night hours…. And create a curfew bell for free blacks and slaves."

The men around the table seem content with the ideas. "That might work," Phillip says, "but we'll have to keep it quiet so that attorney at the courthouse doesn't hear about it."

"Bourge," Johnson adds. "I heard he's planning to marry that mixed-breed girl. He went before a judge to prove she's mixed black and Indian so he could marry her."

"That man has unsouthernly notions of right and wrong," Morgan says. "If he finds out what we're working on, he's going to do his best to interfere just like he has in the past." Morgan looks around at the small group of men he's grown to count on. "We will have to keep our work on these laws in chambers for as long as we can."

On a serene spring day two months later, a congregation sits inside a small wooden church on a hill just outside of Charleston. The preacher, Reverend Brown, a mulatto with graying hair, briskly calls for the remaining guests to come in and find a seat. When the last crowd is inside, the doors closes, he then signals the choir to begin singing. "Won't you let Him in, won't you let Him in. Heist up your window, open up your door and just let Him come on in."

Reverend Brown walks to the pulpit, "This is a day the Lord has made. He done told me everything."

The congregation responds, "Everything!"

"Everything is going to be alright," he continues. "We have two people who will become one before the Lord today."

Richard is stands near the pulpit dressed in a finely tailored suit, eager to see Nicole. The preacher puts a hand on Richard's shoulder and playfully says, "Don't faint when you see her."

The congregation quietly laughs, as the choir begins to sing another song, the front doors of the church open to reveal Nicole. The early sunlight filters into the church, surrounding her with a golden glow.

She wears the prettiest dress she's ever worn, and stands there, her emotions stir, and she wonders how she's going to survive feeling this wonderful. Her eyes fall on Richard's strong face, and her heart is suddenly fuller. With a deep breath, she begins her walk towards him. Richard, overtaken with emotion, doesn't wait for her to reach him. Instead, he walks down the aisle to meet her.

The preacher says, "He had to touch her... to see if she is an angel. "The congregation laughs again.

When the two reach the altar, already hand-in-hand, the preacher begins. "We are here today before the Almighty God to join Richard and Nicole as husband and wife. And so, let it be in the name of the Lord."

Richard follows his French traditions and announces a dedication, "Darling, I will bring my entire heart to our marriage, with all my might. I will do what it takes to create a loving and lasting relationship. We will make it through all our struggles. I will be committed to us and I will create a place for you to have a loving family."

The church rejoices and begins to sing while Richard and Nicole embrace and kiss.

Free people of color, members of the African Methodist Church in Charleston, petition for their church to officially open. They have been attending a mixed Episcopal church, but it did not allow them enough leadership positions.

> *South Carolina*
>
> *To the Honorable…*
>
> *…The petitioners of the subscribed, respectfully sheweth(show) ---That your petitioners are free persons of color, attached to the African Methodist Church, in Charleston, called Zion, and have recently erected a house of worship, at Hampstess on Charleston Neck, at the corner of Chamber and Reed Street--- That your petitioners are desirous of obtaining the permission of your Honorable body to open the said building for the purpose of Divine worship…and that all white ministers of the Gospel of every denomination shall be respectfully invited to officiate in the said church…that no minister of color, who does not reside in the State shall officiate for the said congregation nor shall any slave be admitted a member thereof, without the appropriation of his or her owner, nor shall any person, who is a member of any other religious Society be admitted … without recommendation from the minister of such Society, and (if a slave) the written permission of his or her owner----That every exertion will be used by your petitioners to preserve the utmost order…*

Source: South Carolina Department of Archives and History.

Memorialist are white citizens who are watchful of the whereabouts of free people of color. They know free blacks forge documents but cannot prove it to the courts. Source: South Carolina Department of Archives and History.

> *To the Honorable the President and Members of the Senate of the State of South Carolina.*
>
> *….slaves and free persons of colour, who being able to write, readily manufacture tickets in the name of a fictitious person. It is time the law requires the shopkeeper to prove the authenticity of the permit, but the evidence offered for this purpose by the accuser can seldom be rebutted by the state. The tickets is produced only at the trial, when it's too late to form evidence to disprove its authenticity.*

Chapter 10

Antebellum Church Bells

Church service is just ending at Biggons church, the newly painted white doors open. The slaves are the first to leave. It's populated with prominent whites, who walk out before free black parishioners. The men unbutton their coats, while the women adjust their dresses. A newly married free black couple stay behind to pay their church's secretary the dues to allow them to sit on the front pew.

Some free blacks attend Episcopal churches, which are mostly white congregations. They have recently been considering starting another denomination as the African Methodist Episcopal did in the 1700's, where they would have more leadership roles.

Outside, people gather into small groups. All talking briefly about the service, then about the rumors of a war.

Elizabeth Hargrove opens a small parasol to shade herself from the sun. She is the daughter of a wealthy African merchant sent to the Carolinas to acquire land. After her arrival in St. John's Parish, she purchases Tucker Hill Plantation, and shortly thereafter, marries a white doctor. She has long dark curly hair, dark skin, and is wearing a dress reflecting her status and wealth.

"I worry about my slaves on the plantations," she confides to her friend, Beth Morgan. "If there is a war, they may try to escape to the North, or to some remote area."

Beth tries to be sympathetic. "My husband deals with the slaves, I know little of what's said behind closed doors. I have seen that he's taking more precautions. The overseer now makes sure all the tools are well protected at the end of each day."

Elizabeth gently closes her parasol, "Well, I can assure you that the possibility of war is on everyone's mind. I myself have heard one of my house slaves talking about wanting to see the Yankee soldiers."

Beth looks down, thinking about the future of Troy. "That's bothersome to hear. What do you think the slaves will do if the Yankees come? Will they try to join them?" Beth asks.

"There is concern about the slaves who are allowed to leave their plantations as well," Elizabeth continues. "They move about so easily. I'm considering moving all my slaves to one plantation to keep a better watch."

"This is probably not the best place to talk about this," Beth says abruptly wanting to confide in her fiend, before Morgan makes his way towards them. She's thinking she may be pregnant and it's probably Troy's. If the baby is born a mulatto Morgan will be outraged so she's planning on moving to, Cumberland county, North Carolina for a few months to live with her family. There's a growing number of mulatto families living there. "We have known each other for a while now, and there's no one else to mention it to… it troubles me terribly inside. Maybe soon we'll have a chance to talk. Perhaps—".

Morgan joins the women, "Good day," he says, interrupting Beth before she has a chance to set a meeting with Elizabeth to reveal her long-kept secret about Troy.

"Good morning Sir," Elizabeth responds, sensing Beth wants to end the conversation.

"It was a very fine service…. Yes, the preacher said good words today," Morgan says.

"Yes, he did," Beth agrees, and then turns back to Elizabeth. "We shall see you next Sunday."

A bill of sale shows Caty Lee, a free black woman who purchases a church pew in 1799. Free blacks who pay dues sit in the front of the church.

KNOW ALL MEN BY THESE PRESENTS, *That* J James Mitchell____

for and in consideration of the sum eighteen pounds sterling
______

To me in hand paid, at and before the sealing and delivery of these presents,

By Caty Lee of Charleston, a woman of colour

the receipt whereof I do hereby acknowledge, to have bargain and sold, and by these presents do bargain, sell and deliver to the said Katy Lee (Caty) a Pew at the East Ends of the North Gallery of the said Church, marked with the number one…

TO HAVE AND TO HOLD the said Pew

unto the said Katy Lee (Caty)…

Source: South Carolina Department of Archives and History.

Waitresses walk about a room filled with cigar smoke in a Charleston tavern tending to their patrons. Morgan, Johnson, and Phillip are sitting in the same corner booth, in the back of the room where they always sit. Here, they talk without being overheard. They are deep in conversation, each man's expression fixed with concern as they talk about what's happening in the South.

Morgan stares at the drink the waitress just placed in front of him. "It's almost certain there's going to be a war with the North," he says.

"I agree," Johnson adds. "What are we going to do if the Yankees offer refuge to our slaves who run to their side?"

Morgan gave Johnson a strange look because he said "our" slaves. Johnson, although he could have afforded slaves he'd never owned any. Strangely, he never approved of slavery, maybe because of something he saw as a child. Nor did he support any attempts of free blacks being colonized back to Africa, he just thought whites were superior and should have more than blacks. His father left him an inheritance since he was the oldest; it made him wealthy enough to hold an elected office. Only property owners or wealthy white men could vote in the early years of America.

"Not many slaves know what's really going on," Morgan points out. Free blacks and town slaves are more likely to know. A large number of plantation slaves are unaware of what's going on, and we want it to stay that way. We can do what happened during the Revolutionary War."

In response to the perplexed look on the men's faces, he explains. "The colonist saw they needed more men to fight in the war and offered freedom to any slaves who would fight against the British. Moreover, the

British officers realized it too, so they offered freedom and land to any slave who joined their ranks to fight against the colonists. Most on both sides kept their word afterwards, but not all got freedom or land. Some didn't wait on a decision, they left while they were still free with a gun. If it looks like the war is tilting towards the North, and we need another way to maintain control, we can offer them the chance to fight for their freedom."

"But what happens when the war's over and they want their freedom," Johnson asks.

"Nothing," Morgan said. "There's no doubt that there will be slaves ready to cause trouble after the war, they were born into slavery and will remain. Those who cause any trouble we'll just have to hammer them back into place, like a nail working its way out of a board."

"Besides," Morgan continued. "After we win the war, slavery will be intact. If we gave them freedom, they'll need land and they wouldn't have the resources to buy or work it. Seed costs money. Horses and machinery cost money. No, after the war, it will be easier for the South to recover because slavery is intact."

"What about the whites who agree with the North?" Phillip asks.

"What about them?" Morgan responds with a wave of his hand. "After we win the war, they're free to move up North if they don't like it here.

"I'm more concerned about what the free blacks are going to do," Johnson says. "What do you think they'll do?"

"They'll fight for the South," Morgan said with confidence. "You forget… if there is a war, slavery may be a part of what's going on, on the surface, but it's about who has the power to write laws. What does the North have to offer them? Land? I just don't see it any other way."

Phillip asks. "What if they want to fight for the freedom of slaves? Some slaves are their family members. They may be willing to take the risk of losing everything they have for the freedom of others."

Morgan takes the first sip of his drink. "If I was in their position, I'd want to be on our side. If a free black decides to fight with the North that sounds a lot like disloyalty and the penalty would be the forfeiture of all their rights as a free citizen. We write the laws, and we can see to that." Morgan's ambition has always been to become wealthier, he wasn't going to lose it because of a war.

"But even if they fight for the South, they will still be free, and still walking around for our slaves to see after the war," Phillip said.

"Maybe so but winning the war will solidify the Confederacy… and slavery. Our positions will be intact, and we will continue to control the politics. We will continue to write laws that protect slavery, and our economy. He leans forward resting his elbows on the table and utters with secrecy, "Laws are greater than chains, one law can do the task of a thousand chains."

Phillip pauses and decides now isn't a good time to have Morgan consider the South losing or if a law was written to give blacks the right to vote after the war? It would give blacks the opportunity to gain the majority of political offices in the South.

Johnson and Phillip reach for their drinks, all three men knowing the somber reality in war being at the doorsteps of Charleston.

Chapter 11

Before the Fort Caught Fire

With a blissful look she watches them go in different directions, she pulls her shawl a little tighter, her fulfilment turning to uncertainty. It was a beautiful spring day, but the gentle breeze carries the scent of the burned out remains of the schoolhouse that was just down the road. She'd been the teacher there, until it was set on fire by a group of men. They'd threatened her to say that it wasn't right to teach colored folks how to read. Her responses have always remain the same. "If you burn it down, I will build it again."

A petition was written by the Memorials against free blacks learning to read and write. However, schools exist for their education and most whites tolerate the schools if they were out of sight. These schools increased after the Revolutionary War, some slave owners also allow their slaves to attend.

> *To the Honorable. The President and members of the Senate.*
>
> *The Memorials of the council of Charleston respectfully sheweth that the Grand Jury of Charleston District have presented the number of schools publicly kept for the institution of persons of colour in reading and writing…This law prohibits slaves being taught to write. The facilities however that are afforded them by the means of schools professedly kept for the instruction of free persons of colour, will soon render this knowledge very common in our community. It is impossible to distinguish between the free and the slave of our coloured population and therefore it is extremely difficult to detect violation of this law.*

Source: South Carolina Department of Archives and History.

Two young girls turn back and wave once more before the curve in the road blocks their view. They are Daniel's great-granddaughters. Ruby, the older of the two was doing most of the talking. She took a test yesterday and found out that she'd made a perfect score. She couldn't stop reminding her younger sister about it.

As they turn down the dirt road, Ruby finally gave in to Lyla persistently asking for help with the list of spelling words the teacher had given them.

"Okay! Okay!" Ruby said grabbing the paper out of Lyla's hand and studying the words. Saying, "These are all easy, spell *eight*."

"E-I-G-H-T," Lyla said with confidence. "I have a head for letters," she adds, looking up at her big sister with a smirk on her face.

"Spell the word *south*," Ruby said.

"S-O-U-T-H," Lyla said, and without hesitation started spelling out the next word she remembers on the list. "North is spelled "N-O-R—.""

Without a warning, an explosion thunder and then another. The girls scream not sure what was happening. Lyla looks at Ruby with frighten eyes. "What is that?"

Ruby grips her hand, trying to remain calm. She'd never heard anything like it. Then another explosion rumbles, and both girls take off running towards home. As they ran past the edge of the woods, they could see their Grandma Polly standing on the front steps, and they kept going until she wraps them in her arms.

"What was it?" Ruby asks, trying to catch her breath. "I ain't never heard nothin' like that before."

"Did the sky crack?" Lyla asks.

Polly lets go of the girls. "No sugar, don't worry. You're home now, and that noise is coming from a long way off."

Daniel quickly ran around the corner of the house, easing his pace when he sees the looks on the girl's faces.

Polly looks at him with worry asking. "What do you think?"

Daniel reaches to take off his hat, and then realizes it had fallen off. He scratches his head, his chin pointing to the east. "Sounds like it's coming from Fort Sumter."

"Do you think there is trouble at the fort?" Lyla asks.

The two adults share a look, and the four of them sit down on the edge of the porch. Polly puts an arm around each girl. "We don't know yet."

"But there are people who do," Daniel says, staring off at the blue-grey smoke plumes beginning to appear in the sky. "Things are going to be changing now, but one thing will never change, this has been our land for generations, and we will do what we have to, to protect it."

Another explosion rumbles, now he knows a war has begun. "That's the sound of war," Daniel said grimly.

"I ain't never heard the sound of war before," Lyla said with a shiver.

Inside an open tent at the edge of Colonel Manigault's camp, a locally made flag blows north in the contrary wind. The tent was put up shortly after the Battle of Fort Sumter was launched, like most days after the attack, men of various ages stood in lines waiting to volunteer as soldiers for the Confederate army. Manigault is standing with one of his officers, taking stock of today's recruits while the sounds of the battalion swell behind them.

Horses with a different sound catches everyone's attention and all eyes turn towards the road to see two men riding towards the tent. They're free blacks.

"Sir?" the older of the two recruiters says looking towards the colonel for guidance when he sees them.

Manigault feels the weight of everyone's eyes on him. "There is no law that prohibits free blacks from enlisting and fighting in this war. If those men are free, I just hope they have a good aim with a gun."

"The troubling question is... will they shot at us," the officer next to Manigault says.

William and Daniel P. feel the weight of everyone staring at them. They are the grandsons of their namesakes and are used to the looks. They do what they always do, sit tall atop their horses. When they reach the hitching rail, they dismount and tie up their horses. Both can recall their fathers telling them to protect their land.

The two men look strong and have an air of confidence about them. When they walk to the table, the recruiter asks, "Are you free blacks?"

"Yes Sir," Daniel P. says, responding for both men.

A shadow passes over them and William looks up, shading his eyes against the bright sun to see an eagle circling high above.

The recruiter gives the two a hard look. "How do we know you won't use our own weapons against us?"

"We are here to defend our land against the North," William says. "Our ancestors were here for many generations; this is as much our land as it any bodies."

"We may not be clear about what this war is about," Daniel added, "but we are clear about our rights to protect our land."

A drummer boy steadily taps his drum, held by a strap looped around his back. The troop stand at ease while a soldier carries out the evening roll call. After dismissal, they gather around one of the many small fading fires burning throughout the camp.

An enlistment card for Daniel Peagler Eady in a Confederate Artillery Company. He is identified as a Mulatto on the federal 1850 census.

Source: Fold3.

Meanwhile at the 33rd Colored Troop of SC, Bristow Jr. takes a seat by a campfire close to his tent. It's been a long day and he's tired, there's still enough firelight to read a few pages of a book he's been reading. Susie King the camp nurse, a colored woman requested the books. She'd learned to read while growing up in Savannah, GA now she's teaching soldiers how to read.

It wasn't a book he would have picked for himself, but there weren't a lot to choose from, and he was content to have something to occupy his mind for a little while.

As he thumbs to the spot he last read, he thinks about Anna and how excited she'd been to learn to read all those years ago. He'd been eager to teach her … knowing he had a reason to visit her. They managed to get through a couple of books during his visits with her on the Morgan plantation. Then one day she was gone. He tried to ask her mother where she'd gone, her mother had stopped talking to anyone after they took Anna away. Anna's uncle told Bristow what happened.

One morning before dawn, Morgan's overseer walked into the cabin an early morning while Anna and her mother slept and grabbed Anna right out of their bed. Her mother gripped Anna and held on tight. The overseer broke her hold when he hit her forehead with the butt of his rifle so hard that she fell to the floor, knocking her out. By the time she got to her senses, the overseer had already loaded a screaming Anna into the back of a wagon, her hands tied behind her, and then tied to the wagon so she couldn't jump off. Her mother ran down the long empty dirt road after Anna as fast as she could, but the dingy white horse pulling the wagon was too swift. Still, she'd kept running until she collapsed in the dirt knowing that she would never see Anna again.

It was a long while before Bristow Jr. found out what had become of Anna. Even then he couldn't be sure, people from the church said they heard of a girl like Anna being sold to Pendarvis. It made Bristow's heart ache to think of her there. He remembered his father telling him about the plantation from the time he'd been in the back of the wagon when William and Daniel had ridden past the plantation.

Anna's mother never really recovered, and in a way, Bristow Jr. knew he hadn't either. Anna was punished for wanting to read, and sometimes he felt responsible for what happened to her. If he hadn't taught her, maybe they wouldn't have sold her away.

After a few years, Bristow Jr. decided to strike out on his own and moved to Beaufort, SC. He never forgot Anna, so when it came time for war. Although it was instilled in him from an early age to fight for his land, he knew which side he was going to fight on – the one that gave him a chance to take vengeance on Morgan and see Anna again. He decided to fight for love instead of land.

In his tent the next morning, Bristow Jr. and the other soldiers are waiting for morning roll call. The smell of breakfast serenades their taste buds; bulky flapjacks cook over an open campfire in cast iron pots. While the men wait, they check their guns – even though there isn't any ammunition to load them with – making small talk about family and the things they'd be doing if they were home instead of preparing for a battle, they weren't sure they'd fight.

While they are eating breakfast, the sound of horses pulling a wagon broke through the normal morning noise. Bristow Jr. stood to get a look and saw a wooden covered wagon drawn by four horses, heading in the direction of their camp. There were blue uniformed men on the wagon. There were also four riders on horseback, two on each side with rifles.

The lieutenant in charge of the small caravan uses his binoculars to get a good view of the colored regiment he was approaching. This was his first time delivering a wagon full of guns, uniforms, and ammunition to colored soldiers, and he wasn't at all comfortable with the idea. He also knew the soldiers haven't been paid for months of services. He'd been raised near a plantation with many slaves, and never trusted the look in the eyes of the slaves who watched as he went out hunting with his father. "Looks like the right place," he said to his men. "I can see Colonel Higginson."

When they arrive at the gate, the wagon pulls to a halt. The lieutenant jumps down, and salutes Colonel Higginson, handing him a sheaf of papers. "Sir… these are the uniforms and guns you requested," he says, trying not to look around much. "This is the paperwork that gives an accounting of what we've brought."

Higginson accepts the papers to glance over. When he is done, he motions to the soldiers at the gate. "Let's get those crates off of the wagon and opened to be accounted for," he ordered. The men eagerly unload and open the crates. Higginson look through each crate, making sure nothing was missing. The shipment wasn't everything he'd requested. He signs the papers, knowing he would send a second request.

Word spread through the camp, and men check their rifles with more scrutiny since having ammunition, by the end of the day, more than three quarter of the men are officially armed. His soldiers gather in an open space, Higginson stands atop a tall tree stump, ready to address his men.

He wore a uniform that had yet to see battle. He could see the readiness of the soldiers under his command. These men had left their families and homes to fight for what they believed in. The arrival of the ammunition made them as ready as they were going to get.

"Men we may be under equip," Higginson begins, but I assure you our first battle will be victorious!"

The 1st SC Volunteers are the first Union Army regiment composed of colored soldiers. The commander was Thomas Wentworth Higginson. It is later renamed the 33d Colored Troop of SC. Organized a few months before the 55th Massachusetts, the colored regiment launch the first ground attack against Fort Sumter.

Colonel Higginson and his troops march through a pine forest on their way to Charleston. One of the scouts he'd sent ahead rode towards him. Higginson brought the regiment to a stop. The scout spoke quietly, when he points towards the top of the hill, every soldier turns and looks.

Higginson looks over the terrain, wondering if there were any confederate scouts hiding in the dense forest. Before he had time to consider his options, he heard shouts from the top of the hill. "The Yankees are here!"

The scout told him most of the Rebel soldiers were practicing maneuvers in a field on the other side of the camp, Higginson knew they'd be here quick enough. "Use the trees for cover until you're within shooting range! Jones! Lead the horses out of range," he shouts before joining his men as they begin their slow but steady progress up the hill.

Bristow Jr. peers at the top of the hill from behind the thick pine he'd used as cover on his way up the hill. He was still out of range; with each tree he was getting closer. Soon the sound of gunshots echoes.

None of the Rebel shots land, soon the air fills with dense grey smoke. It provides the cover Higginson's men needs to keep pushing forward.

Bristow Jr. tries not to cough as he takes aim. His first shot as a soldier found its mark, he watches as the gray uniform fall to the ground. Before giving thought to what just happened, he heard a bullet shrill past him and leans back behind the tree. There were no more trees, only the ground between him and the top of the hill. Hand-to-hand battles broke out as soldiers on each side ran out of ammunition or had time to reload.

Bristow Jr. stay low to the ground as he advances. Bailey, one of the men he shares his tent with was to his left. Bailey stops to take aim; he was shot and fell to the ground. Bristow crawls over to him but saw the empty expression and knew there was nothing he could do. His own rifle was empty, so he took Bailey's, determined to finish what he'd started.

With his belly to the ground, Bristow took in the scene between him and the top of the hill. There are fallen men from both sides on the ground. The air was still thick with smoke it was hard to breathe; he stays focus, watching the men at the top, searching for one in particular.

When he found him, Bristow steadies himself and takes aim before squeezing the trigger. The sound of the shot rings in his ears, he saw the man falling to the ground. He'd chosen carefully, hoping the fallen man was the Rebel leader. He'd been right, and when the Rebel soldiers realizes their commander is dead, they begin their retreat, lifting their injured comrades.

The next day, Colonel Higginson and Lieutenant Trowbridge are standing. Higginson knew they'd all been fortunate. Five men were wounded yesterday, only two lost their lives, and the 1st SC Volunteers had been victorious in a battle they'd stumbled upon.

"What do you think the Governors going to say?" Trowbridge asks.

Higginson shrugs. The Governor hasn't given Higginson any battle orders because he hasn't decided how he felt about having a colored troop. "What can he say? The battle found us."

A few months later when the men assemble, Higginson steps onto a small stump to deliver an address.

"For long and weary months, without pay or even the privilege of being recognize as soldiers, you labored on …to strike a manly blow for the liberty of your race…, whose valor and heroism has won for your race a name which will live as the undying pages of history shall endure…

Comrades: nothing can take from us the pride we feel, when we look upon the history of the "First South Carolina Volunteers," The first Black Regiment that ever bore arms in defense of freedom on the continent of America.

Source: Reminiscences Of My Life In Camp, by Susie King Taylor.

A month later, the 1ˢᵗ SC Volunteers march towards another plantation just outside of Charleston. When they reach the yard, Higginson order Bristow and four other men into the main house.

Morgan and his wife hear the regiment approaching, as soon as they saw the dark blue uniforms, they run upstairs to lock themselves and their son Peter up in their bedroom. That was where they kept all their valuables. Morgan quickly empties his pockets and grabs Beth's jewelry, stashing all of it under a loose floorboard next to stacks of confederate money and bonds. He barricades the door with a heavy oak dresser, cursing the fact that as soon as his slaves had heard the approaching regiment, they'd all run out the front door.

One of the soldiers yelled down the stairs that they'd found a locked door, Bristow take the stairs two at a time… hoping. He tries the door it is lock. He knew someone was in the room because he could hear the muffle sounds of a woman crying.

With the butt of his rifle, Bristow smash through the door, managing to knock a stun Morgan, who'd been standing with his bulky weight pressed against the dresser. Bristow and the soldier easily push their way into the room.

Bristow looks around. Beth and her son hid in a corner. Morgan is still on the floor and Bristow can see his eyes blazing, and his hand slowly stretching towards a gun lying on the floor. Bristow took one quick step, kicks the gun out of reach, and glares down at him with his rifle resting on the center of Morgan's chest.

"So, Mista' Morgan," Bristow said, his voice even.

Morgan looks at him, struggling between his usual manner when it came to dealing with blacks and the reality of him lying on the floor at the mercy of a black man in a uniform.

"I bet you don't remember me. I was a boy when I used to come by here on Sunday afternoons. What I really want to know is… do you remember Anna?"

Morgan tried to make sense of what he was asked.

"Come on Mista Morgan. I'm sure if you think hard on it, you can remember Anna. You sold her to Pendarvis, she liked to read" Bristow added, watching a look of recognition cover Morgan's face.

Morgan spoke smoothly. "If you'd left her alone, she wouldn't have been sold. So, you can't hold me accountable for that."

Bristow scowls down at the man he'd waited years to get revenge on. He could end it now.

Morgan didn't have to sell Anna off like she was a sack of seed. If Morgan had been a better man instead of a cruel and calculating slave owner, he could have let her learn how to read.

Bristow felt his finger tighten on his trigger and knew he could do it. It happens all the time. He was sure Morgan wouldn't hesitate to pull the trigger if their positions were reverse, yet he knew there was a difference between the kind of killing that happens in war and the kind of killing this would be if he pulls the trigger.

The smell of smoke was beginning to reach the second floor, and Bristow knew they'd already started the fire.

Bristow relaxes his stance.

Morgan saw him relax. To him, it was a sign of weakness and he made a grab for Bristow's rifle. Bristow easily pulls it out of his hand, spun it around, and uses the butt end to hit Morgan viciously on the forehead the way Anna's mama was hit. With Morgan being out cold, Bristow turns, joins the soldier standing at the door, and leaves the burning plantation house.

A week later, a stylish horse and carriage slow to a stop in front of the Charleston Bank. The bank is close, but a stubborn Morgan who'd survive the fire, knocks louder on the front door waiting for one of the tellers to see him.

A young clerk looks towards the door. "Who's that?" he asks the teller next to him, peering at the man outside.

The other clerk looks. "It's my uncle Morgan," he says, raising a hand of acknowledgement to his uncle, and then leaving to get the bank manager, who hurries to open the door.

"Mr. Morgan... please... come in. How can I help you this late evening?" he asks, a look of concern on his face. With Bristow's attack, he is more determined for the South to have victory. They are winning most of their early battles. "Shall we go to my office?"

Morgan looks at him sternly. "I'm here to invest more of my holdings into confederate bonds."

It was true that many of the banks' customers were investing their money into the Confederacy, but the manager was surprised that Morgan returned. "I can certainly do that for you. Would you like to come in tomorrow morning to get it settled?" the manager asks once the two are alone in his office.

Morgan glares at him feeling the manager was second-guessing his timing. "I can just as easily take all my money out of here and go to another bank."

"No, of course, I'll do whatever you want," the manager says, wanting to appease one of his leading depositors. "I'll be right back with the paperwork." When he returns, he reminds Morgan that he has just over $13000 in his account. "How much more do you want in bonds?"

"All of it," Morgan replies.

The manager reassures Morgan. "And no doubt, you will be a much wealthier man after the war."

Three years later, springtime blooms in Charleston along with the devastation the war had left behind. In a small wooden house that once housed slaves, the windows are propped open with hopes of fresh air chasing out the smell of the decay inside.

A grave faced minister sits on a wooden stool leans towards the man sitting next to him. "He's almost gone."

Johnson discretely trying to catch a glimpse of his pocket watch. When Morgan starts coughing, Johnson stands.

Morgan lay on the bed, his face white as ash. His own coughing wakes him, and when he opens his eyes, they settle on his son Peter, sitting on a chair close to the bed.

Johnson hurries to Morgan's side, holding out the book he'd been waiting to give to him for the past hour. "I brought the journal you asked for."

Morgan focuses on the journal and motions with his left hand. "Give it to Peter. It's his now," he said, his hand falling back to his side, landing on the pile of Confederate bonds Peter had brought to him at his request. They were all worthless, as was all the

Confederate money he'd managed to escape with from the fire. A coughing spasm rattles through his chest, and his hand clutches and crumples the bonds beneath it.

When his breathing was once again calm, he searches the room with his eyes, shortly forgetting that Beth wasn't there. She'd left him the night of the fire. She'd tried to take Peter with her, but his son refused to leave Morgan's side. Months later, Morgan found out that she'd run off with Troy.

"Leave us," Morgan said, his voice rattles with little authority. When the door shuts behind Johnson and the minister, he turns his full attention on his son. "Peter, it's up to you now. This journal, along with the personal journal that's in the top drawer of the dresser, will be all you need to keep my purpose alive. You must...," Morgan goes on, grabbing Peter's arm, "You must carry on the work of preventing the rise of blacks.

"You've seen for yourself the destruction that came with the war against slavery. Charleston has not recovered and won't until slavery is reenacted. We thrived with slavery, and people need to know that truth. As whites, we must maintain certain rights, the war will never end." Morgan sighs and tries to sit up, and Peter helps him adjust the pillows until he was finally able to see out the open window.

"People will look up to you Peter, and with these journals, you'll see how we did it... how we wrote laws that hindered their progress. They were good laws, and it is how God meant it to be" he said, his voice full of conviction. "We controlled them for generations. There is a clear division between the races. It's your legacy to carry on the work of writing laws that will once again solidify our control."

Peter sat straighter and taller in his chair "I will, Father. I will carry on the work."

Morgan stares at his only son, letting the feeling of relief wash through him. With his son's help, his work would carry on.

The sounds of the day came into the room with a breeze, and Morgan watches as people made their way to and from the street in front of his cabin, on horseback, and in carriages. As one open carriage passes by, he sees a hat fly off a child's head and land in the dirt. The carriage stops and a man steps out to retrieve it.

Morgan could hardly believe his eyes. It was Richard Bourge. Morgan eyes darts back to the carriage and he saw Nicole for the first time. There were children in the carriage.

After falling to the floor at the sight, "Help me up," Morgan demands as he moves so he could stand and look out the window again. When he is there, he grips the windowsill and watches Richard tie the ribbon that secures the hat atop the girl's head. The girl shook her head from side to side making sure it would stay on. When it didn't budge, she hugs Richard.

A boy sat next to her. Morgan wonders in disbelief, his heart fill to the brim with anger at what he sees. He should have done more to stop Richard, and that marriage.

His heart pounds. He was gasping for air and falls to the floor again as Peter tries to help him steady himself. He thinks how he had devoted so much of his life against blacks, still not to see his ideal South. Nor the wealth he wanted to gain. The question whirls through Morgan's mind as his wide eyes looks beseechingly into his son's face. *Will he secure my vision of the South?*

No.... Wait! Peter... there's more... Morgan tries to say, but his last breath leaves his body without words.

Colored Dreams

On a misty morning, Bristow sits on the front porch in a chair made by his great grandfather. Sitting in it was always a comfort. It had been a wedding present when he and Anna got married, it reminds him of the importance of family... the family he has here, and the soldier family he'd left behind.

After the war, Bristow's first thought was to find Anna. He knew her mother had died, but he didn't know if Anna knew, so he went to the Pendarvis plantation hoping to find her. A few old slaves were still there, like most of the able-bodied, Anna had left and joined the hundreds of newly freed slaves on their tear-filled journey down crowded dirt roads in search of family.

When Bristow found her, Anna agreed to go back to his family's home. On the long horse ride, they talk, sometimes they journey by foot. She talks about the day she went to the Pendarvis plantation and starts crying, saying she never knew it would be the last time she saw her mother. Bristow puts his arm around her shoulder to reminds her that life will be better since slavery is over.

Anna says, "I was scared when I got there. I was yelled at for not picking enough cotton," she said, looking straight ahead, as they walked. "I was threatened to get whipped, after that I worked hard all day."

"The days were long, and the dried cotton barbs stabbed our hands. We sang to think about other things. At night, we told stories. I heard parents singing lullabies to their children, I tried not to listen 'cause it reminded me of Mama."

Giving her shoulder a squeeze, Bristow says, "You're a free woman now. You can even choose your own last name."

Anna expresses her desire to have a last name, "Most everybody was talking about how good it will feel to have a full name, not only a first name. For the most part everyone decides they would not choose their former master's name, saying it's a reminder of the pain and anguish they want to leave behind. We didn't endure years of misery to have our master's name growing on our family trees. Many decide on Lincoln since he was the president when we were freed."

In the evening when Bristow and Anna reach the settlement, everyone is excited to see them. Months later Bristow's family was overcome with joy when the two decides to stay at the settlement, although it didn't take long for Bristow to realize that he and Anna couldn't settle there.

The war had changed everything. It might have been different if all his kin had come back alive, they hadn't and they fought on both sides. Bristow and Anna move to Beaufort.

Much of Beaufort is in ruins, like Charleston many plantations are abandoned. The ones that remain are nearly the only places to find work.

Four years later, Bristow and Anna had a home of their own, they had eventually moved back to the settlement. Bristow is standing on his front porch during a mid-morning breeze. He raises his head reflecting on how things seem to be getting better across the south. Blacks are being elected to offices and discussions of Alonzo Claflin a minister starting a college in Orangeburg for the newly freed is spreading.

However, the sense of better times didn't last long. After the 15th amendment is written to give black men the right to vote, it infuriates many whites. It was written to prevent political control of the south. Soon thereafter, they forge a movement to keep the new south as the old south. A multitude of malice lands on black folks who wants to participate in the political system.

White folks retaliate and vow the war will never end. Their thoughts of losing the south and its way of life fill their minds, they aren't about to allow black folks to write laws telling them what to do.

They bring their guns to the ballot boxes; this results in many blacks not casting a vote. Although some remain defiant to the consequences, they suffer deadly attacks, sometimes on their entire families. The number of blacks who vote in the elections drop a great extent and the number of elected blacks.

The screen door opens with a squeak, Bristow turns to see Seth, his five-year-old nephew dressed in his Sunday clothes. Seth and his sister live with Bristow and Anna, their father died in the war causing their mother to be unable to provide for them. As always, Seth was ready to make a run for the yard, Bristow was quick to scoop an arm around him before he reaches the porch steps.

Anna held the screen door open for Cora, their six-year-old niece, and sighs with relief when she saw Bristow catch Seth. It meant he would be dirt free for church.

Cora was carrying a small purse Anna had stitched for her, when she held it up for Bristow to see, he could see the joy in her eyes.

Bristow remembers when he was young, he'd rather play on a Sunday, now Sundays, and going to church with his family, was one of his favorite parts of the week. He was a church elder … a respected voice in his church, able to help people in ways he'd never imagined.

The congregation knew his and Anna's story and listen when he talks about the dangers of white southerners who are openly opposed to black people voting and attempts to make progress. He told them protection wasn't at reach for everyone. It was illegal for the newly freed to bear arms, however some former free blacks still had their guns.

Anna talks to the women after church to remind them of their rights. "There was a time when slavery was all we knew. Yet we fought back in small acts of rebellion." Cora often sat nearby listening.

Bristow joins the efforts of the Freedman's Bureau. He encourages the mixed congregation to learn to read and write. At first, it was just the children, as parents watched their children learn to read, many put aside their doubts and began to learn.

In the years following the Civil War.... (the Freedmen's Bureau) aided tens of thousands of former slaves and impoverished whites in the Southern States...

The Bureau was established in the War Department in 1865 to undertake the relief effort and the unprecedented social reconstruction that would bring freed people to full citizenship...

Johnson walks into a Charleston shop several blocks away from his downtown boarding house. He is in his nineties; he comes to this shop on a daily basis to get the newspaper. Without it, he didn't have any way to stay up to date with what was going on. His days in politics were long behind him, ending when Morgan died.

This shop was one of the first to reopen after the war, and he'd started coming here because it was near the courthouse and frequented by politicians in need of newspapers, cigarettes, and tobacco. Most of the politicians knew who Johnson was and were shrewd enough to avoid him. If they didn't, they knew he would take advantage of even the smallest opportunity to start lecturing them on his beliefs about what was wrong with the way things were going in the South during reconstruction.

This morning, his walking cane slips as he was walking out the front door. Fortunately, a strong hand firmly grips his elbow and prevents him from falling. Johnson regains his balance. He was at ease to let the man help him to the bench just outside the shop's door.

Johnson looks up and recognizes the man's face. He was one of the new legislators. "Sit down young man," Johnson commands. "Tell me, how are things going in the legislature?"

The young legislator was reluctant to talk politics with the old man—especially on a Sunday—but was pleased to be recognized and perched lightly on the edge of the bench. A group of black men walks in front of them and a few uniformed soldiers going the opposite way.

Johnson points his walking cane in the direction of the soldiers. "It may appear that the soldiers from the North who were sent to regulate us will be here forever, but a political deal has been made for them to leave. So, listen here," he said, turning his hard eyes back to the young man. "Once they're gone, we can write laws to hinder blacks that will keep them in their place for generations."

The young legislator was speechless and had no idea of how to respond to what the old man said, however it had planted a thought to ponder. Before he had time to compose a response, Johnson gave him a solemn nod, stood, and starts to walk in the same direction as the soldiers.

As soon as Bristow and his family arrive home, both Seth and Cora disappear inside to change out of their Sunday clothes so they could play until supper. Bristow turn and sit on the top step of the stairs. Anna pauses at the door and then join him.

"Every day I thank the good Lord that the war is over, but I swear Anna, sometimes I think it's only over on paper. It's clear that it's going to take more than freedom to be a free man in the south. And what do we want," he asks, looking off into the distance. "All we want is the right to earn a respectable living, and to have equal rights. It's not enough for us just to have freedom. In this new land, we battle laws, too many of our new laws are nothing more than slavery in disguise. Without equal laws, we don't have an equal chance, even our right to own a gun is against the law. We have lived under the illusion that once they saw their wrong, they would do right."

Anna rests her head on Bristow's shoulder. "It may take time, we got that. We have each other, and there aren't any laws that can take that away... least none that I've heard of."

Bristow manages a small chuckle. "You're right, but it's not us I'm thinking about. When I was growing up, my family's land was a symbol of our freedom. We worked our land, and we reaped the harvest. The land is still in our family, so it will always be proof that we are free. It's not the same for freed slaves. They don't have symbols of their freedom beyond the paper promises made to them."

Bristow pauses and says, "Cora went with me to the courthouse yesterday and there was a sign hanging outside, "Colored Entrance" with an arrow pointing to the back. Cora looked and I shielded her from reading it. She wanted to go through the front door as we always did, she kept asking, "Why are we going around back? Then I stopped, deciding to drop off the papers the next time. I don't want her to be influenced by these signs, to make her believe she's not good enough to walk through a front door."

He continues, "There's a malicious intent to these signs, the old laws were ways to keep our numbers from increasing, but the "Black Codes," being called the mighty Jim Crow laws are attempting to do what slavery could not do, make us think they're a superior race. These signs will constantly tell our children they don't belong in the same places as whites, after the signs are gone the messages will remain, unless we tell our stories."

Anna agrees, "The coming generations must know about slavery from our views, they must know we were a strong and mighty people who wanted to read and write these strange words. My mama told me it would lift us up, as it had in Africa, where our people read and wrote their own languages. They must know we wanted to educate ourselves and it was on our minds as we picked cotton, slavery never stopped us from being steadfast."

Seth stands by the open door to his uncle and aunt's bedroom waiting for Cora to finish changing.

"What are you lookin' at?" she asks Seth.

He points. "I saw inside that box yesterday."

"You did?" Cora asks, a look of doubt on her face. "What's in it?"

"It's where Uncle Bristow keeps his hatchet."

"You're lyin', and lyin' is a sin," Cora responds in her big-sister tone.

Seth just shakes his head, then walks into the room, and stand next to the box. His Uncle's work boots are sitting on top of it. Cora looks over her shoulder and listens for a second before joining him. The two stares down at the box.

"His hatchet?" she asks. Her brother nods. She wasn't sure if he was right, but she wasn't going to let her little brother beat her to it, so she moves the work boots and slowly raises the lid.

"Told ya," Seth boasts when the hatchet was in full view. He stares at it for a few seconds and then reaches in to pick it up. It was too heavy for his small hand and slips out of his grip, making a thud when it fell back to the bottom of the box.

"Hey, you two," they heard their aunt call through the front door. "Aren't you coming down?"

Seth and Cora stare at each other in disbelief. Cora let the lid fall shut and cringes when it made a loud noise. Seth quickly put the boots back on top of the box and the two of them race through the house and out the door, stopping short when they realize their uncle and aunt were sitting on the steps between them and the freedom of the yard.

Anna looks at them, and watches their eyes immediately drop down to the porch. "Okay you two… what's going on."

"Seth picked up Uncle Bristow's hatchet," Cora blurted out.

"Is that true Seth?" Anna asks.

Seth lowers his head.

"Seth," Bristow starts, trying not to sound to stern. "You know you're not supposed to touch that hatchet. You're too little right now."

"No, I'm not," Seth pouts.

"How come I've never seen it?" Cora asks.

"Because it's not for you," Anna answers. "We have something else for you. When he's old enough, Seth will get the hatchet. When you're old enough, you'll get something."

"I will?" Cora asks with a smile. She has begun to take on the traits she hears while listening to her aunt at church.

"Uncle Bristow…" Seth starts. "Will you tell me the story about the hatchet again?"

Bristow takes off his hat, "Come sit. You too Cora." They hear a willow bird whilst sitting on the porch. He slowly puts his arms around their shoulders, then reaches for Anna's hand and holds it tight, "We are telling you our stories, so you won't let malicious laws or harsh signs tell you who you are! You must know y*our side of the south.*"

ROSTER OF SURVIVORS OF THIRTY-THIRD UNITED STATES COLORED TROOPS

Sergt. Cæsar Alston,
2d Sergt. Moses Green,
Corp. Samuel Mack,
Edmund Washington,
Isaac Jenkins,
Chas. Seymore,
Frank Grayson,
Bristow Eddy,
Abram Fields,
Joseph Richardson,
James Brown,
Frederick Tripp,
Frost Coleman,
Paul Coleman,
Robert Edward,
Milton Edward.

Source: Reminiscence of My Life in Camp with the 33rd Colored Troops, Susie B. Taylor, company F.

Additional Research Notes

A list of free blacks and mulattoes with the surnames Edy, Eady, Eddy, Edie and Eaddy in SC, NC and GA, who were born free before the Civil War. Their names are compiled from the United States censuses from 1790-1860.

Name	Birth	Lived in	Age	Race
Anne Edy	1770	St. Johns Parish, SC	80	B
Jeremiah Eady	1780	NC	70	M
Mary Eady	1787	St. Johns Parish, SC	63	B
John Edy	1794	Prince George, SC		
Jonathan Eady	1777	St. Johns Parish, SC	73	M
Sophia Eady	1810	Brunswich, NC	40	M
Wm Eady	1808		52	M
Catharine Edy	1802		48	B
Nancy Edie	1800	Cumberland, NC	50	M
Marry Eaddy	1803	Williamsburg, SC	47	B
Francis Edy	1805	Near Pee Dee River, SC	45	B
Sarah Eady	1803	Prince George, NC	55	M
Fannie Eady	1800	St. Johns Parish, SC	60	B
Joseph Eady	1801	St. Johns Parish, SC	59	M
Robert Edy	1812	St. Johns Parish, SC	38	B
Francis Edy	1814	St. Johns Parish, SC	36	B
Agnes Edy	1816	St. Johns Parish, SC	34	B
Alfred Edy	1816	St. Johns Parish, SC	34	B
Jeremiah Edy	1815	St. Johns Parish, SC	35	B
Ransom Edy	1818	St. Johns Parish, SC	32	B
James Edy	1820	Georgia	30	B
Mary Eady	1816	Richmond, NC	34	M
Elisha Eady	1813	Prince George, NC	47	B
Francis Eady	1813	St. Johns Parish, SC	47	M
Louisa Eady	1814	St. Johns Parish, SC	46	B
Zachariah Eady	1814	St. Johns Parish, SC	46	M

Source: 1850, 1860 U. S. Census.

Name	Birth	Lived in	Age	Race
Betsy Eady	1810	**St. Johns Parish, SC**	50	M
Jerry Eady	1815	**St. Johns Parish, SC**	45	M
Maria Eady	1811	**St. Johns Parish, SC**	49	M
Robert Eady	1814	**St. Johns Parish, SC**	46	M
Susan Eady	1823	**Georgia**	37	M
Daniel P. Eady	1823	**St. Johns Parish, SC**	27	M
James J. Eady	1823	**St. Johns Parish, SC**	24	M
Robert B. Eady	1827	**St. Johns Parish, SC**	23	M
Obediah Eady	1827	**Richmond, NC**	23	M
Jeremiah Eady	1827	**Richmond, NC**	23	M
Rachel Eady	1824	**St. Johns Parish, SC**	26	B
Susan Eady	1823	**St. Johns Parish, SC**	27	B
Martha Eady	1823	**Cumberland, NC**	27	B
James Eady	1827	**Cumberland, NC**	23	M
Gabriel Eady	1827	**St. Johns Parish, SC**	25	B
Louisa Eady	1829	**St. Johns Parish, SC**	21	B
Martha Eady	1824	**St. Johns Parish, SC**	26	B
Rachel Eady	1820	**St. Johns Parish, SC**	40	M
Rossana Eady	1822	**St. Johns Parish, SC**	38	M
Gabriel Eady	1822	**St. Johns Parish, SC**	38	M
Betsie Eady	1824	**St. Johns Parish, SC**	36	M
James Eady	1823	**St. Johns Parish, SC**	37	M
William Eady	1822	**Darien GA**	38	C/B

Source: 1850, 1860 U. S. Census.

Name	Birth	Lived in	Age	Race
Catherine Eady	1839	St. Johns Parish, SC	11	B
Lucy Eady	1830	Cumberland, NC	20	M
James Eady	1830	St. Johns Parish, SC	20	B
Henry Eady	1832	St. Johns Parish, SC	18	B
Liezz Eady	1834	Brunswich, NC	16	M
Sarah Eady	1835	Brunswich, NC	15	M
Elly Eady	1838	Brunswich, NC	12	M
TA Eady	1839	St. Johns Parish, SC	21	M
William Eady	1830	Georgia	20	B
Emeline Eady	1837	Savannah, GA	23	M
Phillip Eady	1837	St. Johns Parish, SC	23	M
Margaret Eady	1839	St. Johns Parish, SC	21	B
Thomas Eady	1860	St. Johns Parish, SC	5mths	M
Martha Eady	1830	St. Johns Parish, SC	30	M
Henry Eady	1833	St. Johns Parish, SC	27	M
James Eady	1835	St. Johns Parish, SC	25	M
Diana Eady	1836	Savannah, GA	22	C/B

Source: 1850, 1860 U. S. Census.

Head of Household	Lived in	Free Colored Persons	Race
Charles Eady	St. Johns Parish, SC	5	C
Daniel Eady	St. Johns Parish, SC	1 (7 slaves)	C
Francis Eady	St. Johns Parish, SC	11	C
George Eady	St. Johns Parish, SC	4	C
Jack Eady	St. Johns Parish, SC	10	C
Jonathan Eady	St. Johns Parish, SC	8 (5 slaves)	C
Mary Eady	St. Johns Parish, SC		

Source: 1830 U. S. Census.

Name	Birth	Lived in	Age	Race
Chas Eady	1847	Cumberland, NC	13	B
Ezekiel Eady	1845	St. Johns Parish, SC	15	M
Racheal C. Eady	1846	St. Johns Parish, SC	14	M
Peter Eady	1843	Brunswich, NC	7	M
Willington J. Edy	1843	Cumberland, NC	7	B
Charles Edy	1846	Cumberland, NC	4	B
Sebastian Edy	1847	Cumberland, NC	3	B
Jacob Edy	1842	St. Johns Parish, SC	8	M
Edward Edy	1841	St. Johns Parish, SC	9	M
Maryna Eady	1840	Brunswich, NC	10	M
Henry Eady	1847	St. Johns Parish, SC	13	M
Edward Eady	1840	St. Johns Parish, SC	20	M
Jowler Eady	1841	St. Johns Parish, SC	19	M
John Eady	1842	St. Johns Parish, SC	18	M
Henrietta Eady	1840	St. Johns Parish, SC	20	M
Hester Eady	1842	St. Johns Parish, SC	18	M
Lova Eddy	1840	Charleston Ward 8	20	M
Pompy Eddy	1848	Randolph, NC	12	M
James Eddy	1847	Randolph, NC	13	M

Source: 1850, 1860 U. S. Census.

Head of Household	Lived in	All other free persons
Judith Eady	Liberty, Marion County, SC	9
Molly Eady	Liberty, Marion County, SC	6
Nancy Eady	Liberty, Marion County, SC	7

Source: U. S. Census 1800.

Name	Birth	Lived in	Age	Race
Jane Edy	1853	Savannah, GA	7	M
Charlotte Edy	1856	Savannah, GA	4	M
Sarah Edy	1858	Savannah, GA	2	M
Prince Eady	1850			B
Martha Eady	1851	Cumberland, NC	9	B
Edward Eady	1850	St. Johns Parish, SC	10	M
Thomas Eady	1855	St. Johns Parish, SC	5	M
Victoria Eady	1859	St. Johns Parish, SC	11	M
Salina Eady	1851	St. Johns Parish, SC	9	M
Peter Eady	1856	St. Johns Parish, SC	4	M
Sarah Edy	1856	Savannah, GA	3	B
Alexander Edy	1854	Savannah, GA	5	B

Source 1850 Census.

Head of Household	Lived in	Free Colored Persons	Race
Jeremiah Edey	Brunswich, NC	4	C
Jeremiah Edey Jr.	Brunswich, NC	2	C
John Edey	Brunswich, NC	9	C

Source: U.S. Census 1840.

The surname Eady and Eddy are listed on the 1869 Militia roll in Eady Place, Pee Dee and Bartlett Place as colored citizens.

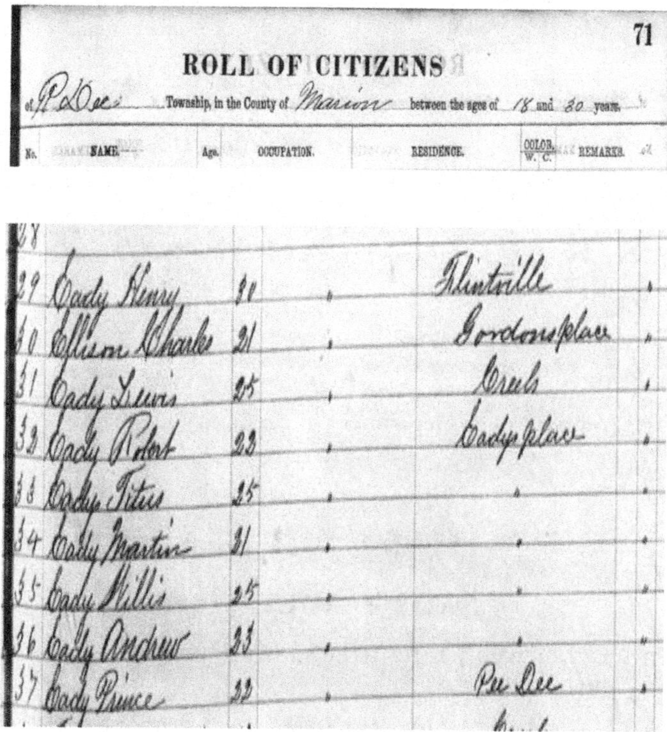

Source: The South Carolina Department of Archives and History.

74

ROLL OF CITIZENS

of *Pee Dee* Township, in the County of *Marion* between the ages of *30* and *45* years.

No.	NAME.	Age.	OCCUPATION.	RESIDENCE.	COLOR. W. C.	REMARKS.
28	Ollison Truce	85				
29	Eady March	15		Bartells place		
30	Eady Jeffrey	40		Pee Dee		
31	Eady Thomas	31		Eady Place		
32	Eddy Peter	32				
33	Eady William	84				

Source: The South Carolina Department of Archives and History.

EADY FAMILY

The term "Other free," refer to non-white inhabitants.

1. Daniel Eady1, born say 1740, received a grant for 100 acres in St. John's Parish, Berkeley County, South Carolina, on 31 August 1774 [S.C. Archives index 2-005-0032-00572; 3-002-013-00327-02]. He may have been the ancestor of

i. James, received a grant for 200 acres in Craven County on one of the branches of Lynches Creek on 8 February 1753 [S.C. Archives Series S213184, volume 6, page 296, item 3]. He was head of a St. John's Parish, Berkeley County household of 1 "other free" in 1790 and 4 "other free" in 1800 [SC:69].

2 ii. Daniel2, born say 1760.

iii. Jonathan, head of a Charleston County household of 9 "other free" in 1800 [SC:69], taxable on 680 acres, 4 slaves, and 1 "free

Black" in St. Stephen's Parish, South Carolina, on 17 March 1825. {S.C. Archives}

iv. George, head of a St. John's Parish, Berkeley County household of 6 "other free" in 1790 and 3 in 1800 [SC: Archives]. He was sued by the executors of Andrew Kennedy's estate on 16 June 1804.

v. John, head of a St. John's Parish, Charleston household of 1 "other free" in 1790 and 5 "other free" in 1800 [SC:69]. He paid tax on 1 "free Black" in Prince George Parish, South Carolina, in 1825 [S.C. Archives].

vi. Molly, head of a Liberty County household of 6 "other free" in 1800 [SC:805].

vii. Nancy, head of a Liberty County household of 7 "other free" in 1800 [SC:805].

viii. William, head of a St. John's, Berkeley County household of 1 "other free" in 1790 and 9 in 1800 [SC:69]. His land in St. John's Parish was mentioned in an October 1825 plat [S.C. Archives].

ix. Judy, head of a Liberty County household of 9 "other free" in 1800 [SC:804] and 10 in Georgetown in 1810 [SC:219].

x. Sarah, paid tax on 1 "free Black" in Prince George Parish, South Carolina, in 1825 [S.C. Archives].

xi. Thomas, paid tax on 1 "free Black" in Prince George Parish, South Carolina, in 1825 [S.C. Archives].

Other members of the Eady family were

Ann, living on Wentworth Street in Charleston about 1811-1817 when she paid the "free Negro" capitation tax [Capitation Tax Book, p.5].

Source: Free Africans Americans in NC, VA and SC from Colonial period to 1820, Paul Heinegg.

Forest Hazel a historian states Jonathan Eady was a "Free person of color," with Indian ancestry:

Jonathan Eady, who is pretty consistently identified as a "Free person of color" can prove to be the nephew of Susannah, George and Daniel Eady. George and Daniel were the earliest Eadys in the Eadytown area, and can be identified as Indian in various affidavits of Indian ancestry …The tribe is not mentiioned, except for the reference to "Catawba," but it seems more likely that they were one of the costal tribes who became known as "Settlement Indians" in the early 1700's...

Jonathan descendants passed into the White race after his three sons served in the Confederacy, most of the rest of the Berkeley County Eadys seem to have passed into the Black race.

…the so called "Smiling Indians," who have now been pretty much absorbed into the general Lumbee community descended in part from the Eady family.

Affidavits with the Eady surname.

William Beamer on an affidavit is identified as a black boy at the age of 12, and in adulthood he personally identifies himself as an Indian. He married Rachel Eady who was considered an Indian and was of dark complexion.

S.C. City of Charleston. 5 Feb. 1822 …Rachel Beamer of Johns Island, of a dark complexion but the descendant of an Indian woman…says that one black boy about the age of 12 years, named William Beamer…

I have always considered myself as of Indian descent… I was born before the revolution about 1762 and fought in the Army of General Greene…. Jane Beamer, Eliza Beamer and Rebecca Beamer now before the court I believe to be my children. Besides these three daughters, he had three sons: John, Joseph, and William. Personally appeared William Beamer and made oath…I I was duly married to their mother, Rachel Eady, by Col. McElney. Said children were born in lawful wedlock. I believe my wife to be Indian when I married her, and…such status has never been denied her. S / William (his X mark) Beamer. Sworn to June 21, 1847, John Williamson, Notary Public.

Source of affidavits: South Carolina Indians, Indian Traders, and other ethnic connections beginning in 1670, by Theresa Hicks.

The Daniel Eady Family were in Berkeley County around Eady Town between Santee Cooper Lakes. There were probably several intermarriages between the Eady's and the Beamers. If the Eadys intermarried with the Beamers, they probably originated in this same area. Hazel's theory is that the Eadys came from the same area. Indian Eadys picked up the name from the Daniel Eady family.

Source: Forest Hazel Historian, at the 4th Annual Southeastern Studies Conference, University of NC Pembroke.

Ulrich Phillips, the author of American Negro Slavery, wrote about the service of John Eady and Austin Dabney in the American Revolution:

Each locality was likely to have some outstanding figure among these. In Georgia the most notable was Austin Dabney, who as a mulatto youth served in the Revolutionary army and attached himself ever afterward to the white family who saved his life when he had been wounded in battle. The Georgia legislature by special act gave him a farm: he was welcomed in the tavern circle of chatting lawyers whenever his favorite Judge Dooly held court at his home village: and once when the formality of drawing his pension carried him to Savannah the governor of the state, seeing him pass, dragged him from his horse and quartered him as a guest in his house. John Eady of the South Carolina lowlands by a like service in the War for Independence earned a somewhat similar recognition which he retained throughout a very long life.

James Eady/Edey a free person of color, petitioned for a plat of land in 1791 to Great Britian, it bordered the land of George Eady..

Transscribed from the land grant below.

> *South Carolina. I do hereby certify for James Eady a tract of land containing one hundred and five acres. Surveyed for him the 10th May 1791 situated in the District of Charleston St. Johns Parish and has such form marks buttings and boundings as the above plat represents. Given under my hand this 6th June 1791.*

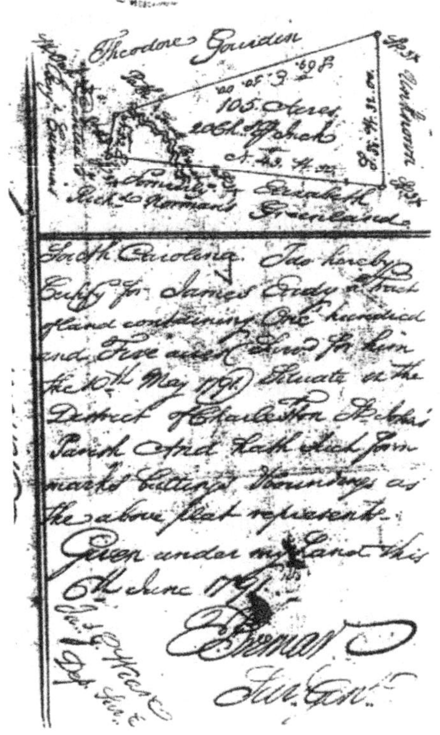

Source: South Carolina Department of Archives and History, a plat for James Eady 1791.

George Eady was listed on the 1800 census as, "Other Free Person." He petitiomed for a plat of land in 1802. *Transscribed from the land grant below.*

> *I do hereby certify for George Eady a tract of land containing two hundred and sixty eight acres. Surveyed for him the 10th day of October 1807. Situated in the District of Charleston of St. John's Parish, and hath such shape from marks and buttings and boundary as the above Plat represents, given under my hand this 5th day of March 1802.*

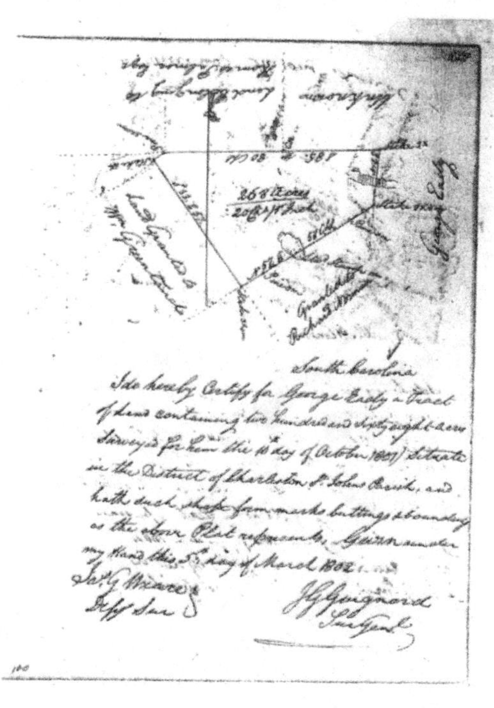

Source: South Carolina Department of Archives and History, a plat of land for George Eady 1802.

George Eady... owned hundreds of acres of land around what is now Eadytown and his residence is noted on an early 1800's map of the Santee Canal. No reason to think it was named for anyone but him and his kin. It had a post office for a while after the Civil War...

Source: Forest Hazel, Historian, North Carolina.

"The African Heritage of American English", author Joseph E. Holloway and Winifred K. Vass who has a degree in African linguistics, wrote, because of South Carolina's primary role in the slave trade it is not surprising to have found 104 Bantu place names. Their research was aided by the University of South Carolina, which provided a wealth of place-names and material.

A map showing Eadytown and several other locations as Bantu named places in SC.

Enlargement from the following map.

Eady Town may have originally been a plantation Negro settlement... now takes its name from the family of Negroes named Eady who predominated in the community. Eady is said to be an Indian name meaning "bad Indian blood" and there is some evidence of inter-marriage with Indians here.

Source: Names in South Carolina, the University of South Carolina.

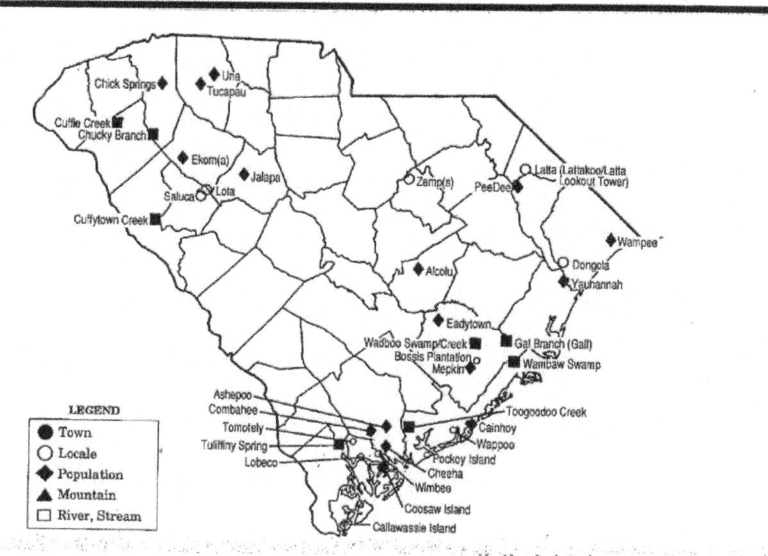

Source: The African Heritage of American English.